The Book Hunters' Apprentice

AIRSHIP 27 PRODUCTIONS

The Book Hunters' Apprentice
© 2022 Barbara Doran

Published by Airship 27 Productions
www.airship27.com
www.airship27hangar.com

Interior illustrations © 2022 Gary Kato
Cover illustration © 2022 Guy Davis

Editor: Ron Fortier
Associate Editor: Gordon Dymowski
Marketing and Promotions Manager: Michael Vance
Art Director/Designer: Rob Davis

ISBN: 978-1-953589-39-2

Printed in the United States of America

10 9 8 7 6 5 4 3 2 1

The Book Hunters' Apprentice

by Barbara Doran

ON CULTIVATION

Book Hunters is heavily inspired by cultivation stories, both written and filmed. It is not an actual cultivation story, as that would need it to focus heavily on the process of cultivation, rather than merely use some of the concepts. However, since the terms I use in this series aren't common in Western fiction I thought it'd be a good idea to discuss the topic and define some of the more common terms.

Note: This discusses fictional cultivation and bears little to no resemblance to the sort of training one finds in certain types of schools. Having little to no experience with such matters, I'm focusing on my fictional cultivation. This author strongly suggests readers interested in such subjects seek their knowledge from a reputable source and not a writer who often tosses whatever she feels like into the stockpot.

OVERVIEW:

Although cultivation is not—strictly speaking—magic, it often resembles magic in its general conception. One could readily substitute the word magic for *qi* in many situations, particularly when it comes to the stage business and props involved. The suspension of belief required for magic is also necessary for the cultivation of the sort I'm discussing.

In cultivation, disciples learn to gather *qi*, or spiritual energy, from different sources. That *qi* is then condensed and stored inside the disciples' physical body, slowly solidifying into a constant source of energy greater than its apparent size.

Most cultivation stories utilize a leveling-up procedure that often resembles a video or role-playing game. It's beyond the scope of this essay to discuss how that came about, although I suspect the concepts are intertwined to some extent. This means a cultivator spends a certain amount of time (how much depends on the cultivator and their access to *qi*) increasing their power until they reach their next level of skill and ability. As might be expected, the difficulty increases each time they level up.

The goal of cultivation is - most often - immortality. There are many different paths a cultivator might take to get there, but in the end, avoiding dying and living pretty nearly forever is where they want to be. Given the increased difficulty, of course, there are many who never make it, for one reason or another.

TERMS AS I USE THEM:

Bottleneck:

When a cultivator is close to the point of leveling up, they may find increasing their spiritual energy creates a blockade that makes that final push particularly difficult. Failure to deal with a bottleneck properly can result in a *qi* deviation.

Breakthrough:

The point where a cultivator manages to push their cultivation to the next level. This is generally an important and dangerous point in their cultivation, as it sometimes will lead to a tribulation.

Core:

Sometimes referred to as a Golden Core, a core is the semi-solidified *qi* energy a cultivator condenses into their *dantian*. It exists as both a physical object and a metaphysical one. It contains all the *qi* a cultivator has absorbed over time and provides them with the energy they need to perform their skills.

Dantian:

There are three *dantian* in the human body, one in the belly, one in the heart, and one in the head. All three are nexus points for one's meridians, but only the lowest *dantian* is safe for human cultivators to use for consolidating their core. Spirit beasts maintain their spiritual energy in the heart *dantian* and certain powerful beings do so in the head *dantian*.

Foundations:

Once a cultivator begins absorbing spiritual energy they need to manage things so their *qi* is properly balanced in both the physical and spiritual sense. Failure to do so can result in a *qi* deviation.

Meridian:

The meridian is the network of energy found in living creatures. Often following or part of the nervous system, cultivators draw *qi* through it to strengthen it and prepare it for when their core forms completely. Damaging meridians can ruin a cultivator entirely. It can also be deadly.

Qi:

This is the spiritual energy cultivators use to perform their specialized skills. Most places have at least a little *qi* but some have huge quantities that are highly prized by cultivation experts. Its nature and effects often vary depending on the location it's found so a cultivator must choose carefully if they don't wish to damage their meridians or give themselves a *qi* deviation.

Qi Deviation:

When a cultivator has a misstep in their efforts to cultivate, whether by some physical or emotional difficulties, failing to properly consolidate their foundations, or even by absorbing *qi* that's incompatible with their type of cultivation, they may have a *qi* deviation. This means the *qi* they've absorbed so far could create a spiritual storm inside them that may result in the destruction of their cultivation and possibly death.

Spiritual Roots:

A cultivator's spiritual roots are generally (but not always) based on the five Chinese elements (Water, Wood, Fire, Earth, and Metal). They indicate but don't necessarily define the cultivator's best choice of spiritual nature. Also, fewer spiritual roots are considered better as a cultivator needs to work with every root fully in order to grow properly.

Tribulation:

When a cultivator makes a particularly difficult breakthrough, the result may be a tribulation. This is generally a test of the cultivator's ability to handle the energies they've just gained. Failure to do so can lead to serious injury or death.

FINAL NOTE:

For more about cultivation stories, I strongly recommend Jeremy Bai's work on the subject. You can find his highly entertaining and informative videos on his channel on YouTube. Search for Deathblade and enjoy.

Chapter 1: A Strange and Sudden Transformation

Human legs made no sense.

For that matter, legs of any kind made no sense. But human legs were surely the worst. Fragile bones connected by stretched muscles and... what was the word? Oh, yes. Cartilage. All covered in a thin layer of skin that lacked even a single scale to protect it.

Then there were ankles and feet. Gods! Don't even get started on those damned things. More bones than a proper set of fins. More cartilage. More skin, none of it thick enough to protect against dirt, stones, and grass.

To be frank, there was little about the human body that felt right or comfortable. It was easily chilled, easily damaged, and incredibly awkward, from the huge quantity of hair pouring down Qing's shoulders to the weirdly shaped appendages to the thing hanging between the legs that just kept getting in the way.

It'd help if he had clothes. But he'd had no time to find any and no time to dress even if he had. Not when he and his precious cargo were being hunted. Not when all he had was speed and endurance and an occasional burst of thunderous *qi* to protect them.

The aforementioned precious cargo moaned, clinging to Qing's neck tightly. Just an hour earlier, he'd been larger than Qing, a human boy ten times the size of a small and well-fed carp. Turned human, that carp was now twice Prince Suzhi's height.

A good thing, too. Otherwise, Qing couldn't pick up his little master and carry him away. Otherwise, he couldn't rescue Prince Suzhi from that would-be thief? Assassin? Even now Qing wasn't sure.

"Qing... I'm... tired. Please. Can we stop?"

Qing slowed enough to look back the way they'd come. No sign of that man, but he'd caught up several times before. Qing had used his newly acquired *qi* to stun him, but he'd never lost him entirely.

If only he knew the way back to the city. His little prince had plenty of guards and sorcerers there to protect him from the stranger. Admittedly, young Suzhi's bodyguards had failed him earlier, falling to the stranger's poisoned darts before they'd had a chance to fight back. The only reason Qing had survived was the fact that he hadn't become human. Yet.

Even now he wasn't quite sure what'd happened. He'd been playing, chasing the pretty bright pebble his little prince tossed for him. They should have been safe enough in the royal parkland outside Khai City. Only family should have approached.

No doubt that was why the guards hadn't been as alert as they should have been. They'd assumed things were safe and had focused more on the amusing sight of a Royal Blue Carp swimming through air as if it were water. They'd paid for their inattention.

What saved young Suzhi had been pure accident. The stone they'd been playing with had been an odd bit of bluish-purple crystal the prince had given Qing a few weeks earlier. It'd seemed an exciting toy, one that'd enriched his *qi*, increasing his self-awareness and giving him small but useful powers. He could swim through air now, chasing around the Prince's courtyard like a small and excited puppy.

Intrigued by his new abilities, Qing and his prince had gone out to play. And when the stranger came after them, Qing had accidentally swallowed the stone, rapidly absorbing its energies and transforming into this peculiar human form out of a need to protect his prince.

The change was permanent. Not the shape - he could take his old shape again if he chose - but he'd never be a mere fish again. The stone had been a spirit stone, as pure as pure could be. It'd increased his self-awareness to full sentience. Increased his cultivation. Increased his power. What had been a spoiled Royal Blue Carp, fit only for decorating a fish pond, was now a dragon carp, with limitless potential, given he could survive.

Sensing the stranger drawing near, Qing put on yet another burst of speed and prayed he - and his Prince - could do just that.

修炼

"Last I saw, they were headed further into the park. I didn't dare follow. I'm not a fighter. If the Prince's bodyguards failed, what could I possibly do?"

Zhi Wenku examined the bodies scattered around the stream, then the only survivor, Lady Feng Lai. "How did you escape?"

The royal tutor pointed at a large tree. "I was behind that when those men attacked. All I could do was hide while the naked one grabbed our prince and that fish and ran."

That fish, as Lady Feng put it, was the reason Zhi Wenku had come to Khai City. The King's Consort, Xia Lan, had been her student once. She'd sent for Zhi Wenku, concerned by the sudden change that'd overtaken her youngest son's favorite pet. Zhi Wenku - as a scholar, a bookseller, a Master of the Zang Shanghu sect - might have some explanation for what'd happened.

They should have kept both prince and fish inside the palace, but she wasn't surprised they hadn't. Her former student had been a rowdy outdoorswoman who'd constantly run off to avoid her lessons in Jing'ling Forest. As far as Zhi Wenku could tell, this particular son was just as impossible to tie down.

She gave herself a brief moment to wonder just why one of the abductors had been naked and what had actually happened. Lady Feng's story was practically incoherent, mentioning a flurry of darts, sudden death, and a flash of light that'd half-blinded her.

"Master Zhi? What should we do?"

Zhi Wenku turned to the speaker and his companion; palace guards who'd accompanied her to find the prince and his pet. "One of you take Lady Feng back to the palace and report. You'll need someone to collect the dead and more to help search for the prince. The other should stay here."

"But... Third Prince Suzhi...."

"I'll hunt for him while you bring help." Zhi Wenku drew her whisk from her sleeve and let it enlarge a foot or so before setting it floating a few inches above the ground. "With luck, I'll find him and his abductors before he's harmed."

Lady Feng rushed over and clasped her hand. "Please, Master Zhi. Please take me with you."

The last thing Zhi Wenku wanted was to deal with a helpless innocent in need of protection, not with another to rescue. Something about the way the woman looked at her, something about the way she clung, made Zhi Wenku relent. "If I tell you to run, you run. If I tell you to stand, you stand. And if there's a fight, you hide."

"Yes. Yes! I will. I will!"

Zhi Wenku stepped onto her whisk, enlarging it just a bit more so Lady Feng could stand behind her. "Hold tight and don't panic." They rose high into the sky, Lady Feng clinging just a bit too tight.

"What... what are we going to do?"

Zhi Wenku reached into the side pocket of her backpack, sliding her fingers into her Warehouse. A tool carried by every master of the Zang Shanghu, it was a Spiritual Space containing anything from one to several dozen rooms. It was combination of storage and shelter, depending on how it was needed.

Focusing her thoughts on the device she required, Zhi Wenku grasped gently and brought out a delicate-looking dragonfly, carved of jade and bamboo. As it fluttered over her palm, she said, "Prince Suzhi is protected from scrying spells, just as he's protected from poison and most small magics. You said he had his fish with him, right?"

"I'm not sure. It may have been killed in the attack."

"Based on what I've been told, I doubt it." Zhi Wenku traced the symbols for 'search' and '*qi*' over the dragonfly's body. "From what King's Consort Lan told me, it sounds like the fish came into contact with some sort of powerful *qi* source. My tool may be able to find it, given the park's magic doesn't overpower its senses. We'll just have to see."

"I... don't understand. What *qi* source?"

"No idea. That's why I was sent for, though. To investigate the fish." King's Consort Lan had noticed her son's favorite carp changing, gaining abilities he ought not to possess, given he was just a heavily spoiled baby fish. Cultivation usually required time and effort and Qingqing had expended neither, as far as anyone knew. "This isn't the time for a lecture. We have to hurry."

Focusing her attention on the dragonfly, Zhi Wenku gestured. "Well. Get to work. We don't have all day."

She just hoped she could save the prince and his little pet from his abductors before it was too late.

修炼

The worst part of the energies Qing had absorbed was the fact that they kept increasing. He'd consumed almost half the stone's *qi*, he sensed, but there was more to come. If he weren't using what he had to protect himself and his Prince from their enemy's darts he might well have been injured.

He couldn't feel their pursuit right now but he couldn't be sure they'd escaped. They needed a safe place for his prince to hide in, in case Qing lost control. Right now all they were doing was getting further and further from those who'd protect his Prince. If he overloaded and died there'd be no one to keep young Suzhi safe.

"Little master? We're near that mountain like you said. Where should I go now?" He peered at the jagged rocks and carefully trimmed trees, reflecting that the place seemed too perfect, even to an ignorant carp with ambitions.

The boy peered up at him, arms wrapped tight around his neck, legs tight around his torso, his robes the only thing protecting Qing's frontside from the rushing wind as he ran. "There's a cave maze... my grandfather had it built."

Qing had no idea why anyone would build a cave but he didn't understand humans well at all. A maze might be useful to lose their pursuit. Given that, of course, they could avoid getting lost themselves. He followed his Prince's directions up a narrow path to a cliff-face pockmarked with dozens of openings.

"Third entrance from the left leads to a garden," the Prince gasped. "And a little house."

A garden. A house. Inside a cave. Beyond a maze. Qing definitely didn't understand humans. Still, he ran into the opening and was displeased to see small lights light up above them as they passed. "That's going to lead him right after us," he complained.

"They only stay lit where there are people," Prince Suzhi told him. "Don't worry. Just run."

Running was almost too much for Qing. But he did as he was told and rushed along the smooth pavement, letting his Prince guide him whenever they came to a choice of paths. Up two ramps. Down two more. Left and right, two times. That led them to an empty room whose walls were covered with spirit beasts.

"Let me down," Prince Suzhi ordered and limped painfully to the wall once Qing obeyed. "Let's see. Ah. Here they are." He pressed one of the beast's heads, then another. A *bixi* and an *ao*.

Quite suddenly the whole room dropped down, fast enough that Qing stumbled and nearly fell. Prince Suzhi did fall, lying panting on the stone as they slowly went down and down and down.

"Little Master!"

"It's all right. Just... wait. Almost there."

If Qing weren't exhausted and ready to just sit down and do nothing at all, he'd have struggled to join his Prince. Instead, he stayed where he was, not daring to sit for fear he wouldn't get up. Until at last the room jerked to a stop and soft light gleamed through the doorway from which they'd entered.

Now Qing went to his Prince and - despite young Suzhi's protests - helped him stand. "Can... can you walk? I don't think... I can carry you."

"I'll manage."

They stumbled slowly through the doorway into an impossible garden. Qing was sure grass and trees and flowers shouldn't grow inside a cave, yet there they were. A small cottage perched beside a lotus-covered pond created by a slow and rippling stream.

"There... there should be something for you to wear... inside."

"Something to take care of Little Master's leg while we're at it," Qing countered. That damned assassin hadn't reckoned with the Royal Spells when he'd hit Prince Suzhi with a poison dart, but that just saved the Prince from the poison. He had to be hurting badly by now.

They stumbled into the cottage, both desperately yearning for a chance to just lie down and rest. Both well aware they didn't have time. This room might be safe. Might be protected. But that assassin had proved determined and relentless. Qing didn't know how the man kept catching up but he didn't dare assume they'd lost him.

Not when his Prince's life was at stake.

修炼

Zhi Wenku's dragonfly headed straight for the nearest and most powerful spiritual *qi* in the area. The only trouble was, that she wasn't sure that *qi* came from Prince Suzhi's fish. The royal parklands had been built and added onto for centuries, with each subsequent architect and gardener trying to outdo the last, both with plants, animals, landscape, and magic.

That last was the main problem. While *qi* wasn't exactly magic and magic wasn't exactly *qi* the differences tended to blur in Khaitan. That meant the sorcery used to build the royal parklands could be mistaken for a spirit beast's natural *qi*.

Still, she'd have to check, just to be sure. The Prince's abductor may have deliberately hidden in the Quiet Peaceful Mountain to obscure the *qi* the fish had absorbed. Though, thinking on it, she wondered how he could. You had to be a member of the royal family, a royal servant, or a guest to enter.

"You didn't recognize either of the men involved in the attack, right?"

Lady Feng denied the idea quickly. "I couldn't have recognized the one with the darts. He was masked. And the one with the strange tattoos, the naked one, was a total stranger."

That last was particularly odd. The masked one was clearly an assassin. But why would the other, the abductor, run around entirely unclothed? An idea flickered and faded. She'd have to consider the matter later.

"We'll have to search the caves, even so. The Prince may have been forced to let his captors inside."

"But... how? We're not family."

Zhi Wenku eyed the woman, wondering at her ignorance. "You're Third Prince Suzhi's tutor. That makes you one of those permitted into the mountain."

"You aren't, though! You can't possibly send me in there alone!"

As if Zhi Wenku had ever intended such a thing. She landed at the lowest cave entrance and helped Lady Feng down. "King's Consort Lan gave me the permissions I need. I can go anywhere in the park."

As Lady Feng faltered over the news, Zhi Wenku sheathed her whisk in its slot on her backpack and took the woman's hand, walking determinedly straight past the protective wards. Inside the cave, tunnels were white polished stone, designed to resemble the purest of pure mutton-fat jade. It was beautiful, in an overly elaborate sort of way.

"I don't suppose you know the layout of this place?"

A nervous look around. "I've never been here," Lady Feng admitted. "I've heard rumors of a special room, though. Something called the Nightless Grotto. The King's father built it for his Consort."

It sounded like something Lian Kaitian would do. The previous king had been something of a romantic, fond of grand gestures and sneaking off with his wife for private time. "Do you know where it is in here?" The tutor shook her head at the question and Zhi Wenku sighed. "Well then, I'll just have to send my dragonfly to... what the...."

She said further words because someone was shouting somewhere outside. Zhi Wenku frowned. "Who's that, I wonder?" Had the King's soldiers arrived already? It seemed unlikely.

Lady Feng stepped to the entrance, listening intently. "I think it's Guardsman Lao. The one I told you about. The one who went chasing after the prince?"

How had Zhi Wenku forgotten about him? Something didn't make sense, but she couldn't quite work out why. "I wonder how he's so far behind us if the Prince actually is inside?"

A shrug. "We took a direct route. Maybe that damned bastard left false trails?"

Surprised by the vulgarity, Zhi Wenku raised a brow. "I didn't know tutors were allowed to be so frank."

Taken aback, the tutor bit her lip. "Apologies, Master Zhi. It's been a difficult time. I forgot myself."

She had indeed. "Never mind. We should find Guardsman Lao and coordinate. No point in revisiting old ground if it isn't necessary."

As Lady Feng agreed, Zhi Wenku called her dragonfly back and changed its target to the source of those curses. If it really was this Guardsman Lao they might as well regroup and start searching more efficiently.

Besides, all that noise he was making risked scaring the abductor into taking more dangerous action than he had so far. They couldn't risk young Suzhi's life just because some poor fool couldn't keep his mouth shut.

Even as they headed off to find Guardsman Lao, however, Zhi Wenku couldn't help feeling something was wrong. She just didn't know why.

修炼

Prince Suzhi hissed as Qing dealt with his injury. Removing the dart was difficult and Qing feared he'd left a barb or so in the wound. They'd have to wait for someone who knew what they were doing. All Qing could do was clean and bandage the wound, using crystal clear water from the waterfall, strips of silk torn from bedding, and a healthy influx of *qi* energy to hasten the healing.

"I'm sorry. I don't know how to do this better."

"It's all right, Qingqing. It'll be fine. Father's healers can fix what's left. You don't have to use your *qi* on it."

Honestly, Qing did. Every use of *qi* lowered the surging tide of energy rushing through his body. He needed that respite if he was to make it through this and get his little master to safety. "Don't worry," he promised. "I have enough."

About to say more, the prince suddenly paused, looking at the wall behind Qing. "There's someone else in the caves."

"How can you be sure?"

Prince Suzhi pointed. "That."

'That' was a scroll painting showing an image of the mountain. To Qing's surprise, tiny dots of light moved around the surface of the painting, two together, one separate. "What is it?"

"A scrying scroll. Turn the peonies to change the image."

"Just a moment, then." Qing finished bandaging his prince's wound and cleaned his hands, reveling in the purity of the water as he did so. It'd be so nice to swim in that pool, instead of trying to stay upright on these awkward human legs. Shoving the complaint aside, he went to the scroll and found a group of peonies carved into the frame.

Turning one flower caused the image to shift, seeming to cut into the mountain and show bits and pieces of the tunnels. A bit of fiddling with the other peonies adjusted the position of the image as if one were flying around the mountain, above it, or even inside.

If they weren't in such trouble already, Qing would have happily played with the painting for hours, just to see how it worked. He forced himself to focus, following the source of two of the light spots and finding two women walking through the tunnels, painted images surprisingly clear.

Neither were familiar, although that meant nothing when one was originally a small fish from a small pond. "Who are they?"

Prince Suzhi frowned. "I've seen the younger one, the one with the pack before, but I can't remember when. The other... That's one of the palace servants, I think. Gods know how she ended up here."

Qing shifted the image again, finding the source of the other light. "Not good," he muttered when he found it. "That man again."

"He can't get in, though. The guard spells only let people with the royal tablet inside."

The royal tablet was the carved stone pendant worn by the royal family or their trusted servants. "It let me in," he pointed out. "And I'm naked."

Prince Suzhi giggled. "You should do something about that," he pointed out. "And you were let in because I'm with you."

Somehow Qing wasn't sure that made for good security. But he didn't argue, just went to the closet and pulled out some of the clothing Prince Suzhi had said he could borrow. As he fought to get the pants on, Prince Suzhi limped over to the painting to keep an eye on the others.

"These things are impossible."

"You'll manage."

"I'm too tall." Why the hell was he so tall, anyway?

"Not really. Father's much taller than you are. So's mother."

Qing snorted. "I was five inches just an hour ago," he complained.

"Who told you to eat that stone?" By now Prince Suzhi understood as much as Qing did about what had happened to him. "Er... are you going to be all right?"

Truth to tell, Qing didn't know. He felt bloated, the occasional crackle of lightning flowing through the blue and silver markings that'd once been his scales. "I'll be fine," he reassured his prince, even so. "Why are these things sliding back down?"

"Come here. I'll tie the belt." Once that was done, they both gazed at the painting again, finding the two women and realizing the pair had met up with their pursuer. Even worse, they'd brought the man in, as if he were their ally. "Qing... I'm scared."

"I'm scared too," Qing admitted. He eyed the garden, "Can they reach us?"

"Not without my permission."

Then the best thing Qing could do would be to distract their pursuers and make them chase him, instead of trying to find his little Prince. "All right. You have food and water and you're safe here. You stay and I'll make them follow me."

Prince Suzhi didn't like that. "You're my pet fish. You should be under my protection, not the other way around."

"I'm a dragon carp," Qing retorted. "I have more *qi* than I know what to do with and I'm faster and stronger than you. Now you do as I say and wait here where you're safe."

"But...."

He went to his knees, catching his Prince's hands in his. Such an awkward movement, bending joints in impossible ways. "Please, Little Master. You've guarded and raised me all my life. Let me return the favor. Let me be the one to protect you."

After a long moment, Prince Suzhi agreed.

修炼

Zhi Wenku felt off. Something, some forgotten thing, niggled at her. Niggled and tried to work its way to the surface of her memory. Whatever it was just kept slipping away. She forced herself to concentrate. Failed. She could tell there was something wrong with Guardsman Lao, but not what. He seemed all right in his black clothes and scraggly beard. He even smiled pleasantly enough.

Still unsure of her reaction, Zhi Wenku asked the man, "Did you see much of the man who took Prince Suzhi?"

"Far too much of his bare ass, I'll tell you that much."

Given the man had been naked when he'd shown up and attacked... wait. That wasn't right. Lady Feng had said something else back at the stream. She'd said... something about an assassin with darts. The same darts that'd killed Prince Suzhi's guards. What else had she said?

Zhi Wenku's dragonfly buzzed, the sigils on its wings brightening. Startled, Lady Feng jumped back and away, asking in a worried voice, "What's wrong with it? Is it going to break after it hit the wall so many times?"

"No. That just means it's picked up the energy again." They'd been exploring the passages of the cave system for almost an hour, her tool trying to go through solid stone again and again because it couldn't find a direct route to the *qi* it sought. "It's built to take a beating."

"Seems to me you should have designed it to follow a trail," Guardsman Lao complained.

"You were following the Prince's trail. Haven't you spotted it yet?"

That silenced him momentarily. Then, "I thought I found it earlier, remember? But it went straight into a dead end." He paused, looking around. "The same dead-end we're headed, for now, you know."

Zhi Wenku hadn't noticed. She wasn't a tracker, being more accustomed to following trails of knowledge inside books and scrolls. Tracking living people was what the guardsman had been trained for. She eyed him dourly. Again she found herself convinced something was wrong here and couldn't tell why.

No. She knew why. She was just having a difficult time working her way to acknowledging it. Something was definitely wrong but what that wrongness was just wasn't coming to her. She knew better than to set the thought aside, no matter how much part of her wanted to, but it was hard to find time to stop and think about it when she had to find the Prince.

To cover her confusion, Zhi Wenku eyed the passage. "How can you tell we're headed for that dead end from before?"

A sigh. "I left marks along the way. See?" Guardsman Lao tapped a thin scratch in the polished surface of the wall. "We've been here before. It ends in a stone wall."

"Should you be defacing your King's property like that?" Zhi Wenku asked dryly. As the man glared at her, she added, "And it isn't ending in a stone wall this time. Look." She pointed ahead at an opening into a large room, one with an elaborately carved wall on the far side.

As they entered, a soft voice said, "I've been expecting you."

The speaker was just a bit taller than Zhi Wenku, with a terribly young face that hardly seemed properly lived in. He wore pale silk underclothes - pants and a loose-fitting short robe - and a sheer loose outer robe that slid halfway down his shoulders as if he'd no idea how to keep it in place.

He also held something that glowed and crackled between his fingers as if he'd caught a ball of lightning in his bare hand and clutched it tight.

"You rotten bastard. Give it back!" Lady Feng snapped, stepping forward, even as Zhi Wenku tried to work out just what 'it' was. "Thief!"

"You want it?" The young man smiled broadly as he tossed what he held towards them. "Try to catch it!"

As a small storm flew through the air at them, all Zhi Wenku could do was block its path with her whisk and hope she was fast and strong enough.

修炼

Rapid cultivation had a number of drawbacks, especially not knowing how to settle all the *qi* rushing through one's body. If Qing hadn't been using most of that energy to escape, he would have lost control. Would have exploded in a horrifying mess of flesh and scales.

Even now, after running so far and striking out as often as he could, Qing knew he'd be in trouble soon. As long as he kept fighting he'd be all right. But no one could fight forever and sooner or later he was going to have to do something with all that energy. He just didn't know what.

Fortunately, he could put it off for a bit. The woman with the white jade whisk was fast and skilled, a perfect target for someone who didn't want to hurt or kill anyone. She didn't even need talismans to protect herself from his lightning strikes; just sigils drawn rapidly in the air between them, inky marks that somehow managed to glow despite their color.

Qing's real problem was the other two. The prince had said the woman was a palace servant, but she seemed to be more their attacker's ally than the prince's. As for the man, he was definitely the assassin who'd murdered Prince Suzhi's bodyguards and tried to abduct the prince himself.

He dodged a strike from the whisk; long strands of pale fiber glittering iridescent in the soft lighting. Not horsehair he was sure. Dragon whiskers? Kirin mane? Qing wasn't sure how he guessed at such things but he probably shouldn't let himself be distracted.

A dart almost struck Qing, evaded only in the last instant by a flick of his sleeve. He was getting better at this being human thing. Better at moving and evading. Not fighting, though. A kick from the servant-woman sent him rolling across the room.

Again he gathered his *qi* into his hand. Again he formed a ball of lightning. That forced his attackers back, as they tried to decide what he was going to do with it. He seized the respite to ask, "What is 'it' that I stole?"

"You know what 'it' is, you damned interfering bastard!"

"Actually," the woman with the whisk said calmly, "I'd be interested in knowing what 'it' is as well. Particularly since you seem to have forgotten who we've come for."

The servant bit her lip, looking frustrated. "Yes... Yes, of course, Master Zhi. Where's the Prince, murderer? What have you done with him?"

Murderer? "I haven't killed anyone!" The very thought appalled. "That man there's the killer!" Qing pointed at the assassin, who sneered at the accusation without bothering to deny it.

"No one?" The woman with the whisk, Master Zhi, eyed the servant. "Lady Feng, I feel as if your story has been changing."

Lady? That made no sense. Qing would freely admit to not knowing a great deal about human customs but he was pretty sure 'lady' wasn't the title for a mere palace servant. He was about to say as much when the woman called Lady Feng turned on Master Zhi.

"I was hoping to hold the delusion in place longer," she admitted grimly, as light and shadow flickered over her body, changing her appearance from one blink to the next. The woman who stood there now had the same face as before, but her plain brown clothes turned black, just like the assassin's. "Deng Zhou, get that thing off the little bastard. I'll take care of our interfering bookseller here."

With that, she drew a long flexible blade from her belt and launched herself at Master Zhi.

修炼

Clarity struck fast, now the woman calling herself Lady Feng gave up trying to cloud Zhi Wenku's mind.

It was embarrassing that the spell had worked at all. Zhi Wenku might have been pardoned for accepting the story initially, on her arrival to a bloody scene with one hysterical survivor. But the woman, whoever she was, had been tangling her lies ever since.

The first lie, that she was a trusted tutor, disproven by her ignorance of the royal playland and her vulgar language. The second lie, that a dart-wielding assassin hunted Third Prince Suzhi through the royal park, transformed into the claim that the man was trying to save young Suzhi from his abductor. And the third lie, that this boy had been the one to kill the guards when his only weapon was a powerful and poorly controlled blast of *qi*.

Swatting 'Lady Feng' away, Zhi Wenku shifted so she could guard the young man's back. "This one is Zhi Wenku, of the Book Hunter's Sect. And you?"

A moment of silence, followed by the crackle of lightning as the boy sent his attacker flying with another ball of energy. Then, "Qing."

Qing. "That's all?"

"That's all."

"So you're *zhi* as well." Her family name didn't mean 'just' but the pun was too easy and she was in a mood. Behind her, young Qing groaned and she chuckled. "Never mind. Focus your attacks better. You're barely bruising your opponent."

"I don't know how."

He didn't know how? What sort of cultivator was he, to be so completely lacking in the most basic skills? Before Zhi Wenku could help him, though, she had to deal with her own opponent. Preferably before she was skewered.

Seeing the blade aimed for her forehead, Zhi Wenku flicked the hairs of her whisk around 'Lady Feng's sword, a move that had the woman cackling triumphantly. "If you want that damned thing cut to pieces, be my guest!"

Zhi Wenku flicked the strands of her whisk tighter, twisting them around the flexible sword beyond its ability to bend. Another flick of the wrist slid the hairs free, dropping the ruined weapon to the ground. "Did I say my weapon was plain horsehair?" she asked.

"You haven't since I've known you," young Qing said pertly, tossing yet another poorly developed lightning ball at his opponent. Darts flew at him, only to be caught in the boy's sleeve. "Hey, cut that out. Haven't you learned they don't work on me?"

"Don't argue with your enemy. Get that *qi* under control before you deviate. Didn't you pay attention to your teacher at all?"

"Teacher? I don't have a teacher."

'Lady Feng' threw a handful of caltrops at Zhi Wenku, more to distract than to injure. It almost worked, but Zhi Wenku brought her arm up to block the high kick aimed at her skull. Grasping the woman's ankle, she twisted, a sharp, bone-shattering move that elicited a shriek from its victim.

Dropping 'Lady Feng' to the floor, Zhi Wenku turned her attention to young Qing. "No teacher? You don't learn to use *qi* without some help." She used her whisk to snag the next few darts, sending them flying across the room. Seeing the boy wasn't interested in explaining and having no time to waste, she moved at the man called Deng Zhou and was surprised

"FOCUS YOUR ATTACKS BETTER."

when all he did was evade her.

Now there was focus. Attacked by a better fighter and thus endangered, Deng Zhou ought to have at least defended himself. Instead, he kept his attention on young Qing, as if the youngster were the only important target in the room. Now, why would that be?

The memory hit suddenly. There'd been so many things happening in the last few hours that she'd been distracted, too busy saving the prince to remember why she'd come to the royal court in the first place. "You're that carp!" If nothing else she ought to have noticed the pattern on his skin.

"You say that like it's a bad thing," Qing retorted. "I'm the most beautiful and precious carp in my Prince's pond."

"You're the only carp in your prince's pond," Zhi Wenku grumbled. Why were spirit beasts like this, anyway? Always bragging about themselves, once they cultivated up to self-awareness.

Deng Zhou leaped at the boy... the carp... fingers suddenly sharp in a way no human's could ever be. Startled, Zhi Wenku moved fast, wrapping her whisk's strands around the man's neck. A sharp tug jerked him backward, just as young Qing leaped atop him, entire body crackling with whatever *qi* it was the silly fish had absorbed.

Soundlessly, the assassin fell limp, smoke rising from his body in a way that shouldn't be possible. As the man's skin charred away, revealing the shattered shape beneath, Zhi Wenku realized just what was wrong.

He wasn't a man at all. He was a puppet built of ceramic, leather, and steel.

修炼

The assassin's death sent a chill straight through Qing. "No. Wait. I didn't mean... I didn't want... I didn't...."

Master Zhi's gentle hands grasped his shoulders. "Child," she said, though she hardly looked more than ten years his senior. "It's all right. Look closely."

He stared at the body underneath him. "I... What is he?"

"A puppet of some sort." Master Zhi helped Qing to stand. "A mechanist's work it looks like."

Qing had no idea what that meant. Nor was he in any state of mind to tell. *Qi* still surged in his body, wilder now the fight was over. Maybe fighting had been a bad idea? His situation felt worse, not better.

Unaware of Qing's confusion, Master Zhi turned her attention to the other woman, who'd lain silent and still for the last few minutes. "Another puppet," she muttered. "Amazing spellwork." She reached out, about to examine the woman, only to jerk her hands back as the thing set to twitching wildly.

Something about those motions scared Qing. Despite the haze of confusion created by his rapidly deteriorating condition, he flung himself at Master Zhi and covered her with his body, blocking the explosion he somehow knew was coming.

He was barely in time, as the second puppet shattered, shrapnel slamming into his back painfully. If he weren't already confused and dazed by whatever his *qi* was doing to him he would have been in agony. As it was, the pain provided an unexpected focus that almost saved him.

It wasn't quite enough. Likely he'd have been destroyed by his poorly controlled *qi* if Master Zhi hadn't pushed him off her and set her hands to his temples. More *qi* entered his system, moving calmly and smoothly as opposed to the tempestuous energies already there.

He tried to push her away, scared of what was happening. She forced him to sit upright. Sent her *qi* coursing through his meridians and somehow showed him what to do with the damned stuff. He stopped fighting, following the woman's lead, accepting her guidance.

"You cultivated too fast. Acquired too much *qi* at once. You have to build your foundation now."

None of that made much sense to Qing at the moment but he let her show him the path. Pulled his *qi* in as she told him, focusing it deep in his belly. Oh. Yes. That was right. That was so very right. It came together; a slowly solidifying warmth that seemed to expand into something he ought to be far too small to contain.

At last, he let his excess *qi* drain into that core of warmth, leaving just enough to flow through him and maintain his meridians. He opened his eyes, looking into Master Zhi's concerned face. "I... yes. Thank you."

"Eh. I couldn't let my grand-student's pet fish blow himself up with a *qi* deviation." Master Zhi sighed, sitting back. "Speaking of whom, where is young Suzhi, anyway?"

A small voice spoke from one of the animals carved on the wall. "Grand-student, ma'am?"

Master Zhi chuckled. "You're in the garden, then? Good. That's safe enough." She helped Qing stand, checking him over and tugging bits and pieces of that other puppet from his backside. "You can stay there if you don't trust me, of course, but just so you know, I'm Master Zhi Wenku and

I used to be your mama's tutor when she was just about your age."

Before Qing could suggest they just wait for the royal guards to come fetch them, because he was sure they would, the room slowly lowered down, summoned by his little master.

修炼

The King's guards arrived at the cave to fetch the three of them home an hour later. "We'd have come faster if we'd known where to look," Guard Commander Ban told his prince apologetically. "Fortunately someone noticed the garden was in use."

They reached the palace, and the King and his Consort's worried arms just around dinner time. As they ate, Zhi Wenku explained the situation to Prince Suzhi's parents. "Young Qing's sudden increase in cultivation is due to a stone Prince Suzhi brought home last month. It appears to have been a spirit stone that ended up in a stream on Tengli Khen."

That made King Lian Kaijian eye his son. "Are you supposed to take things from that mountain?"

Defensively, Prince Suzhi offered, "It wasn't anywhere near the shrine, father. It wasn't even on the mountain."

Zhi Wenku smiled wryly, having already expressed her opinion of that excuse. She continued, "I hesitate to guess why, or how, those two puppets became involved. But their creator must have sent them to retrieve that stone."

"There was a theft at the shrine a month before A-Zhi visited," Xia Lan said, brushing her fingers through her son's hair when he tried to object to the baby name. "A set of carved spirit stones offered by the Duke of Houttan. But the piece A-Zhi had didn't look carved."

Zhi Wenku couldn't say for certain, given young Qing had accidentally swallowed the stone during the attack on his prince, but, "It was in the water for some time. No doubt it'd already begun releasing the *qi* stored inside. Just as well. Small carps that swallow spirit stones are lucky the only thing that happened to them was a sudden elevation to dragon-carphood."

That made young Qing flush, high color offsetting the brilliant blue and silver scale pattern along his neck and temples. They'd have to teach him how to hide that if he proposed to do anything more than return to his pond. "I didn't know."

While the price of ignorance was often high, Zhi Wenku chose not to belabor the point. She continued her explanation. "That theft at the shrine may have been instigated by whoever created those two puppets. I've no idea why it took them so long to realize they'd lost part of the offering, but they must have traced it to Prince Suzhi. The puppet calling herself Lady Feng used delusion spells to make people think she belonged to the palace, no doubt hoping to steal the stone back."

"But I was keeping it with me," young Qing added. "I didn't know it was increasing my cultivation, of course, but I liked it."

If Zhi Wenku had arrived just a day sooner or told her former student to keep the pair in the palace, none of this would have happened. Unfortunately, it hadn't occurred to her that there'd been more to young Qing's change than mere spirit beast cultivation.

"I took him with me to the park because... well...."

"Because he's your friend and you wanted to play," King Kaijian chuckled. "And I gave you permission, so you're not in trouble for that. Just for not mentioning where you got that stone."

The Prince flushed. "Sorry, father."

"We've already gone over that." King Lian Kaijian waved off the apology. "Master Zhi, please continue?"

"There's not much more to say. These two went out to play and the would-be thieves took advantage of the chance to steal the stone back. The one calling herself Lady Feng used her spell to distract the guards so her partner could murder them. They didn't plan for young Qing to swallow the stone and have his spiritual energy increased. He's fortunate it didn't kill him."

"They startled me," young Qing protested. "I had it in my mouth when they hurt my prince!"

Zhi Wenku ignored the youngster. "When he turned human, young Qing escaped with Prince Suzhi, the male puppet in pursuit. The female must have stayed in place to confuse any rescuers. She didn't reckon with my ability to search for the Prince directly. I am, however, embarrassed to admit that she managed to confuse my understanding for a time."

"You still worked it out," the King told her, eyes sharp with worry as he looked at his youngest son. "Thankfully."

"What happens now?" Xia Lan asked.

Lips tight, Prince Suzhi bit into his steamed bread, refusing to look at anyone. His reaction made both his parents raise their brows. "Son?"

"Don't want him to go."

"Little Master, we talked about this."

"Still don't want."

The tired and fussy voice of a ten-year-old protesting reality failed to change it. Zhi Wenku waited for him to fall quiet before saying, "Young Qing's been transformed. What should have taken him years, even decades or centuries, to achieve, he's cultivated in less than an hour's time."

That much the King and his wife both understood. "He's unstable." "At risk of losing control and *qi* deviating."

"Exactly. I've sealed what's left - about half - of that spirit stone. It's almost enough to bring him to tribulation. But he's not ready to attempt it. The divine thunder of the Dragon Gate is nothing to scoff about, even for a dragon. If he's to survive, he needs training, a great deal of it."

Zhi Wenku had discussed this with the youngster and his little master back in the garden. Neither were happy about it. Not because young Qing didn't want to learn. Not because his prince wanted him ignorant. But because the sort of training Qing needed meant he couldn't stay here.

"What needs to happen, then?"

"I've been asked to leave Khaitan to hunt books outside our borders." Far from the punishment it sounded, it was an acknowledgment of her strength and talent. Only the best masters of the sect could become true Book Hunters. "Up until now, I've put off choosing an apprentice. I simply haven't needed one. Outside of Khaitan, a second pair of hands, or fins, and a second pair of eyes will be useful."

Young Qing's eyes widened, their color darkening as the irises broadened out with emotion. "You mean...."

"I would offer you a place as an apprentice Bookseller, child. You'll have to do a lot of walking and a lot of training to catch up, but if you're willing to take me as your master, I'll teach you what you need to know."

Only a moment of hesitation slowed the youngster's reaction. Then he was out of his chair and on his knees, bowing deep. "Master Zhi," he said quietly, earnestly, "I am barely out of my egg, but I will do my best."

Zhi Wenku set her hand to the boy's shoulder. He was young. Inexperienced in the ways of the world. Ignorant in ways a human child would never be. He was also brave and determined and industrious. He might not be the perfect apprentice, but then she hadn't been either, back in the day.

He'd be a challenge. A problem. A Master's curse upon their student.

She was looking forward to it.

Chapter 2: Old Forgotten Things

Qing was bored. Bored and lonely. Bored, lonely, and about ready to break Master Zhi's rules. Again.

It'd be nice if he had Master Zhi's cabinet walking skill. But that was a talent she'd only recently cultivated. All Qing was, was a dragon-carp cultivated halfway to full dragonhood. Right now he wished he was just a carp again. Then he wouldn't be expected to dust.

"Really, we have access to the Zang Shanghu's entire spell collection. Surely there's something in there that could clean."

"The last apprentice who tried to use magic to finish his chores wound up nearly drowning himself," Master Zhi said from behind him. As usual, she always seemed to sneak up just as he was saying something particularly foolish.

He huffed, sending a cloud of dust spinning through the air. Another huff sent that cloud into the waiting basket to join the rest. He'd have to empty it soon. "Am I out of the carp bowl yet?" he demanded. "I didn't mean to make trouble last case."

"You make trouble every case, little fry. Chasing that astronomy book through the governor's mansion was just your usual nonsense. Besides, you're not dusting for punishment. You're dusting because we need to move the books to make room for more."

He turned. Stared. Realized how worried his master looked, her narrow brows drawn together in a frown. "What happened?"

"Elder Lang contacted me; we're needed on an emergency collection. Younger Brother Tackachul has fallen. We're to find his Warehouse and fetch it back to Khaitan."

Master Tackachul? That nice old spirit beast riding the northern circuit? But wait, "What about Apprentice Matcha?"

"Gone too."

A wave of sorrow flooded Qing and he almost turned carp and leaped into his bowl to hide. He controlled the urge. "How much space will we be needing?"

"He didn't have much compared to us, but his most recent recovery may have something to do with his disappearance. Whatever we find of his possessions will need to be quarantined. We'll need three standard-sized rooms, full security."

Thanks to her cultivation, Master Zhi's Warehouse was one of the largest in the sect, but most of the rooms were just eight by eight feet square and some were only half full. Quarantine meant a room had to be completely emptied, cleaned, and warded, which meant shifting the books around. And shifting the books around was a problem in itself. Some books just didn't get along with others. The last thing they needed was the silly things quarreling.

"I'll get working on that, then," Qing said, and set to doing exactly that.

修炼

Compared to their usual circuit, the North was a desolate waste of broad, empty, rolling hills. When Qing complained, Master Zhi scanned the hills ahead of them. "It could be worse. We could be in the desert." As Qing shuddered at the thought, she nudged her pony, Jangle, forward. "Don't fret. We're leaving as soon as we find Brother Tackachul's Warehouse."

"We know it's safe, right?" Qing knew the answer to that question, but he couldn't help fretting. A Book Hunter's Warehouse was created through spatial magic. Most *qiankun* items - bags and sleeves and boxes bigger on the inside than out - couldn't be physically entered or lived in. Only the most skilled crafters could create a spiritual space the size of a building inside a backpack. Master Zhi's Warehouse could be even smaller if she chose; a true triumph of the art.

"According to Elder Lang, it is. Of course, it took us three weeks to get here since we got word. Gods know what's happened since then. We're almost to the spot he last reported in."

True. Elder Lang knew Master Tackachul and his apprentice had fallen almost as soon as he'd failed to check in; the tattoos they all received made sure of that. She'd have a general idea of his location from his nightly report, but anything could have happened in the time between then and their loss.

It was too bad they'd had to travel afoot the whole way. Master Zhi had a flying device - a crane puppet big enough to hold a half-dozen people - but she didn't want to attract attention. The world outside of Khaitan wasn't entirely friendly to magic and cultivation.

"I believe we're getting close," Master Zhi remarked suddenly.

Qing peered across the hills, sniffing the air. Nothing but the smell of grass and flowers and... "There's a river. And a lake."

Master Zhi frowned. "I know your sense of water is superior to mine so I won't ask if you're sure. But the map says there's only a pond that way."

"Then the map is wrong."

She agreed. "In which case, something else is wrong as well. Our maps are usually accurate." She unrolled the thing in the air between them. "You see? There's a stream that runs through this area and a pond, but no river or lake."

"Could this have something to do with what happened to Master Tackachul and Apprentice Matcha?"

A light pat on his head. "Don't jump to conclusions. It might be. It might be something else. Until we get there and see, there's no point speculating. Stay sharp. Even if this has nothing to do with our lost ones, it's still worrisome."

They continued along, Master Zhi riding, Qing walking beside her. Ponies, even specialized beasts like Jangle, wouldn't carry a dragon carp like himself. He didn't mind walking, though; it gave him a chance to practice his long steps. It'd be useful for when his carp form developed limbs, a change he sensed was coming soon.

The scent of water grew stronger and stronger and Qing could feel its movement ahead of them. Yes, definitely a river. Definitely a lake. Its depth was impossible, though. "Are you sure we're where you think we are on the map?" he couldn't help asking.

That got him swatted and deservedly so. An apprentice shouldn't question their master's judgment. It wasn't a hard swat, however, possibly because, "I keep wondering the same." Master Zhi reopened the map to compare the actual landscape against the faint glowing image in front of her. "Except I don't think there could be two mountains with that shape and that shrine."

The mountain in question was a mile away, its smooth slope contrasting with the more jagged ones behind. There was a carving, a man holding an eagle, just like the one on the map.

Qing touched the spot lightly, listening to the spell repeat the name, Green Mountain Peak. It said nothing more, not even the name of the God carved into its side. "I wonder if it's important."

"It's important to someone. Whether it matters remains to be seen." Master Zhi put the map away again. "Let's keep moving. Whatever it is we're heading for, I'd rather we got there before it's too dark to do anything."

The road curved up a steep slope, giving them a view of what lay beyond. Qing couldn't help saying, "I said it was a lake. And a river."

"Indeed you did," Master Zhi sighed. "I never said I disbelieved you."

She dismounted, gazing dourly at the water. Nor could Qing blame her. The river he'd sensed rushed smoothly between two hills through a vast expanse of impossibly flat lake water. It seemed shallow and so clear the grassy surface of the land below was obvious as if the water wasn't there at all. Only the reflected sky proved otherwise.

"How deep?" Master Zhi asked, knowing he was the expert in such matters.

"I'll have to touch it." Qing might often be impetuous and foolish about mysterious things but this took uncanniness to a level beyond his endurance. "I'm not sure I...."

"You have protections and I promise I'll pull you back if it looks like you're in danger."

Trusting his master, Qing walked to the edge and carefully set his hand in the water. He stretched his senses, examining the lake's depth and width, searching for life.

It took a while. There was so much water. Too much water. He found himself being drawn back suddenly, Master Zhi looking worried. "Are you all right? I was afraid you were losing yourself."

"Not lost, no. Just overwhelmed." Qing took a deep breath. "Remember how I was, the first time I saw the ocean?"

She eyed him. "You're not telling me it's as big as that."

"Not by width, but it's deep. Too deep. There's a chasm towards the center. Right about where Master Tackachul and Apprentice Matcha last reported in."

修炼

They circled, checking for signs of life, both near the water and in it, finding nothing. Animals, birds, and insects; all seemed to avoid the lake. As far as Qing could tell, there were no fish. "It's uncanny."

"It certainly is." Master Zhi eyed the water distastefully. "Fetch my diving pearl. We're obviously going to have to go in."

Entering that too still, too deep, water didn't appeal. "Maybe we should send for help?"

"Until we have a better idea of what we're facing sending for help is a waste of resources."

Like most working Book Hunters, Master Zhi was an independent soul. She'd request help if she knew she was outmatched. She wouldn't admit a job was too much for her without even trying. "Yes, ma'am."

She swatted him again, knowing without him saying just what he was thinking. "Don't sass me, child. Hurry up. And put Jangle away while you're at it. He won't like it underwater."

Leading Jangle inside the Warehouse wasn't easy. The pony never liked being put away and generally needed bribes - in the form of eggs - and a great deal of petting. Long practiced at dealing with the pony's moods, Qing got him inside, threw a basket of raw eggs into his feeding bin, and closed his stable door. Then he fetched the diving pearl and rejoined Master Zhi.

By this time she'd found a squirrel hiding in some nearby bushes. She was using her translator earring to communicate, listening to the little brown beast's chirps with intense interest. When Qing approached she fed her informant a fat acorn and sent it on its way.

"Anything useful?"

"Not much. Apparently, everything happened overnight. The little one says she went to sleep in her favorite tree and found herself stranded the next morning." Master Zhi pointed at a small island covered in small trees. "Luckily for her, she could leap from branch to branch back to dry land."

That must have been terrifying for the little one and Qing said so. "Did she touch the water at all?" It was one thing for a dragon carp to stick his hand in. Quite another for a mundane beast.

"It scared her so much that she didn't dare. Though she says her tail got soaked and she took no harm."

That was good. Master Zhi's diving pearl had limitations. It could only protect from real water. If the lake had anything dangerous in it, the pearl would be useless. For that matter, Qing's scales wouldn't stand up terribly well against certain substances.

"I don't think there's any acid or the like in there," Master Zhi pointed out, seeing his relief. "You would have noticed just now."

That was true. "If anything, it's pure. Too pure. Even the small lives you usually find in water are missing."

"Then the only thing we can do is go in and find out."

Qing folded up the Warehouse and - at Master Zhi's gesture - put it in his sleeve. Then he waded into the water, transforming into the largest koi he could be, opening his gills and taking a breath. It tasted strange, like nothing at all, but it was breathable. Relieved, he flapped his tail at his master.

Master Zhi joined him a moment later, diving pearl surrounding her with a faint gold glow as she walked down into the deeper water. Her voice echoed softly back to him, "Go slowly and tell me if the water changes at all."

They moved towards the chasm, Master Zhi walking, Qing swimming. In the bright daylight, the landscape seemed perfectly normal, as if Qing were flying over the grass. It was a pleasant sensation. Pleasant and a little distracting.

"Look sharp," Master Zhi pointed. "We're at the edge."

They were indeed. Qing rose up in the water, so he could see further ahead, then dropped to the grassy lakebed. "It's a perfect circle," he reported.

"Can you see the bottom?"

"No. It's too dark. Like someone spilled ink."

Master Zhi sighed. "Our only choice is down. Be ready for anything. If something happens to me, get our Warehouse back to Khaitan and send an Elder."

Qing understood and didn't like it. She wanted him to put his life over hers and that wasn't the way things should be between master and apprentice. But she was right. Their primary purpose was to protect the books they'd collected and recovered. Qing, smaller, faster, and a far better swimmer, had the best chance of surviving to bring help.

He just hoped he wouldn't be called upon to do so.

修炼

The only way down was to swim, which meant Qing had to let Master Zhi ride him. They'd done so before, that time they'd visited the ocean, but he'd found it undignified. Undignified and embarrassing; he hadn't wanted a repeat.

This time he found her presence on his back oddly comforting. She wasn't heavy even on dry land. In the water he could barely feel her. Only the tug on his mane and her slight movements told him she was there.

"My night-pearl isn't bright enough," she complained, waving the softly glowing jewel as she spoke. "I can barely see a few feet."

Qing couldn't see much at all. Carp eyes were fine in full daylight, but in this darkness, he was better off using his barbels to find his way. His were quite long, too; some were even half the length of his body. He used them, and all his other senses, smelling-tasting a familiar odor. One he slowly recognized. He paused. "Squid ink."

"Not good. Not good at all, especially given Tackachul's true nature."

Qing understood Master Zhi's worry. Master Tackachul was a spirit beast who'd cultivated to human form. His true shape was some sort of sea creature, one of the multi-limbed beasts that squirted ink. Had Master Tackachul run into trouble and created this mess? Had he played with something he shouldn't have?

"Which book was it he'd found?" Qing set to swimming downwards again.

A grumble. "How am I supposed to know if he didn't bother telling Master Lang?"

Master Zhi hated feeling ignorant, so Qing didn't push the point. Just kept swimming down and down. He startled at one point, feeling as if he'd bumped into something soft. When he looked for it, it was gone.

"What is it?"

"No idea. I can't see anything. But something touched me."

"Move more slowly and let me know if you feel it again."

It happened several more times, only to have the thing disappear into the surrounding darkness before he could get a good view. He fought back panic, focusing his attention, and was startled when he smelled other, more interesting flavors. Tastes that reminded him of Chang'an's bustling market: Dumplings of all sorts. Sausages. Breads. Glazed fruits.

Sounds came next. Faint but growing louder. Voices calling. Someone singing. A *qin* being played. It didn't make any sense and he tried to listen closer, drawn toward the noise and smell like a small child.

That was a mistake. He should have swum closer to the edge of the chasm walls, not gone towards the center. Unable to see clearly, focused on the strangeness, he almost swam straight into a huge pagoda, the tower barely visible in the black mist-filled waters.

An arrow shot past him, slowed by the water but still dangerous. Startled, afraid, he dodged sideways. Evaded another. And another. And finally had one scratch past his fin, the sharp sting making instinct take over. He dove down and straight through a barrier between the water and the bubble of air beneath.

Without water for support, they fell, tumbling through the air and landing atop a wooden cart full of vegetables of questionable freshness. Unable to breathe, Qing gasped for water, flailing wildly, sending the things scattering across the ground.

As he struggled back to human form, dimly aware of Master Zhi checking him anxiously, an old man's voice said in an odd mix of Chinese, Tartar, and Khaitanese, "You're paying for those cabbages, you know?"

修炼

Qing worked himself back to normal while his master paid off the cabbage seller. Luckily merchants in this strange place accepted silver nuggets because they certainly didn't have any of the cubes the people here used for money.

Once Qing was human again he looked around, staring wide-eyed at a lantern-lit city street. Red lacquer wood buildings in an ancient Khaitanese style framed the curved street, suggesting the road circled around this small city.

He turned his attention towards the middle, where a huge pagoda stood. It was the one they'd run afoul of earlier, its elegant materials and colorful hangings telling him the thing had to be important.

"My thanks for your forbearance," Master Zhi told the old man. "Hoping you forgive us."

The old man counted the silver nuggets with a pleased expression. "That's all right," he told her. "Quite all right. Really all right." He paused. Eyed her thoughtfully. "Strangers to Ziyou City, obviously. You want help getting around?"

She thought about it. "I wouldn't mind taking some time to sit and drink tea, perhaps discuss this town and its ruler. You do have a ruler, of course?"

Sticking the last of his cabbages away, the old man scoffed. "We got rules. No gossiping to newcomers." He eyed them. "Used to be we'd get 'em more often, 'bout every month. Slowed down, though. Hasn't been any since ten years back, when that lot of sheep butchers showed up."

Qing fought the urge to comment that the old man was gossiping right that moment. It wouldn't be politic to do so. No point in shutting down the font of information before they'd filled their jars. "You did ask if we needed help getting around," he offered diffidently.

"Weren't me who'd be doing the helping. You'll want th' Guidance Department." The old man pointed down the road. "It's... hmmm, you could go either way and get there just as fast. But there's someone y'could be talking to that side of the city, if yer thinking on staying."

Master Zhi considered the suggestion. "Very well," she agreed. "We'll seek out this person you mention and hope they can help us." She cupped her hands. "Much thanks for your forbearance and again, apologies for our sudden and crushing arrival."

修炼

They followed the road clockwise, Qing staring at everything with bright and obvious curiosity. Under some circumstances, he'd hide his awe better. But he and Master Zhi had found their job easier if he played the innocent naïf whose ignorance of the world desperately needed to be rectified. One could learn a great deal that way, but Master Zhi was too cynical and worldly-wise to manage it.

To Qing's surprise, no one cared that a pair of total strangers wandered their streets. No one approached and no one avoided them. Qing wondered why. He'd learned to expect human curiosity and nervousness in the face of strangers.

"Do you think the sheep-butchers that old man mentioned were from a local tribe?"

"Hmm. Possibly. I'm seeing the right sort of decorations for steppe nomads. And some of the people here have the right look, aside from being a bit pale. They can't be the same ones as those Master Tackachul had been visiting. The old man said they'd shown up ten years ago. One wonders how they got inside, with all that water above us."

Which returned them to the question of how this place was created and whether something Master Tackachul had been carrying had something to do with it. Or, perhaps, it'd been with the nomad clan he'd stopped with?

It took half an hour to get from one side of the city to the other. Not because the road was that long but because they kept having to stop and let people by. This place really was quite crowded.

Noticing a familiar design on a banner, Qing pointed it out to his master. "Isn't that attractive? Should we find out who wove it? For trade?"

Master Zhi eyed the banner. "It is, indeed, fascinating," she agreed. "We'll investigate it later." Her expression showed she understood Qing's concern because the banner bore an intricate and long-disused design. Three characters written in an ancient talisman script. Spirit. Knowledge. Strength. The insignia of the now defunct Sanzan Sect.

Once, a long time passed, Sanzan had been a respected sect formed of three sub-groups. Zan Jing'ling, the Spirit Being Sect. Zan Zhihui, the Knowledge Sect. Zan Techang, the Strength Sect. Together they'd worked to protect their particular focus from being lost.

Unfortunately, Zan Jing'ling had overstepped its bounds some centuries ago. Instead of simply protecting spirits and magical beasts from the dangers of the human world, they'd taken to abducting and imprisoning them in what they called a sanctuary.

To add to their crimes, they created a secret society within Khaitan's borders. One intended to take over and control all families involved with magic and cultivation. Already annoyed by their holding unwilling

"NO ONE APPROACHED...THEM."

spirits captive, the king at the time ordered the Zan Jing'ling to disband. No surprise the sect rebelled, forcing its sibling sects to choose between loyalty and law.

Zan Zhihui and Zan Techang chose law. Not out of fear or infidelity but because of Zan Jing'ling's actions. If they hadn't been imprisoning unwilling and harmless spirits. If they hadn't killed those who defied them. If they hadn't attempted to assassinate the king. So many ifs and so many wrongs.

In the end, while Zan Zhihui and Zan Techang survived, they chose separate paths and took new names. Zang Shanghu, the Book Hunters, and Techang Dao, the Warriors of the Way. Still friendly, still willing to help the other, but no longer bound in lock-step.

For a symbol from that long ago time to be here, as pristine as if it were woven yesterday, was a peculiarity atop a host of other peculiarities. Qing had no idea what it meant and - from her expression - neither did Master Zhi. They'd have to investigate after they'd learned more about this place.

Their destination was easy to find and quite large. Banners on either side of the door proclaimed its purpose, 'Guidance Department', written in beautiful gold script on dark red cloth. The huge red doors were open, revealing a great hall with more banners and people going back and forth.

Master Zhi led them inside, not pausing a moment to ogle the decorations. She didn't bother looking at the people busily working at their desks either. They looked like officials doing paperwork, as far as Qing could tell. Nothing odd or noteworthy about them.

Realizing he was gawking, Qing hurried to join Master Zhi at the large old desk at the far end of the room. A young woman sat there, reading a scroll with an intent frown. She looked up as Master Zhi arrived, eyes narrowing.

"Well," she said sourly. "It took you long enough to find us."

Qing was about to ask just who the woman was to be expecting them at all when he recognized her bracelet. He'd seen it at the last Conference, gracing the wrist of the fifteen-year-old girl who'd just been named Master Tackachul's apprentice.

Looking at her face, he could see the outline of that same girl in somewhat older features. It was impossible, or ought to be, but this was their lost comrade Matcha, aged ten years in the space of a few weeks.

The question was, how?

修炼

Almost immediately after she'd acknowledged them, Apprentice Matcha ordered tea be brought to her private office. Only when they'd been served and privacy seals had been activated did she turn to Master Zhi. "It's been over ten years. What took you so long?"

Qing realized his fellow apprentice's appearance had a reason and blurted, "It's not our fault. We arrived just a few weeks after you died... wait. You didn't die. Master Zhi, if she's not dead, why did it seem like she died?"

Master Zhi settled gracefully in her seat and sipped her tea, pretending Qing didn't exist. "My dear girl, did your Master come across one of the Books of Time? And if he did, was he foolish enough to try and use it?"

"Don't you 'my dear girl' me. I'm full grown now!"

"Oh, I very much doubt that. Years don't make the adult, after all. I should know."

"You're annoying."

"Indeed. But unless Younger Brother Tackachul named you a Disciple, which he shouldn't do without confirming it with the Sect, you're still just an apprentice."

The pair sniped back and forth at each other for a minute or so longer, giving Qing time to examine the room. Well decorated but not overly rich, it had a half-dozen styles from a half-dozen eras. Scanning his memory, he thought the oldest piece was a good five hundred years old.

Waiting for his Master and Apprentice Matcha to finish would take some time. Matcha was Master Zhi's several times great grand-niece as well as Sect Niece and they had similar personalities; including their fondness for pulling at each other's ankles. Qing sighed. "That Qiongqi statue comes from Qishan and hasn't been carved that particular way for at least five centuries."

"And your point, you rude little fish-faced brat?"

Stifling the urge to argue that having particularly large eyes and a constantly bemused expression did not make him fish-faced, Qing told her, "That's just before Sanzan Sect disbanded. Are they here, still in one piece?"

She scoffed. "One piece? That's what they'd have liked you to believe."

Thoughtfully, Master Zhi asked, "But they are here?"

"They were. Or, rather the men's side was." Apprentice Matcha waved a hand. "They'd been fighting their captives for decades. Used to rule half of Ziyou city before we arrived. Master Tackachul made a deal with the beast spirits and helped chase the Zan Jing'ling disciples out. What do you think all that black stuff is overhead?"

"That really is his ink out there, then? He trapped them in it?"

"Five days after we arrived. He told me to wait for help and took our Warehouse to set up a shield array. All our diving pearls are in there, so I couldn't leave the city to wait up top, either."

Now Qing understood, sort of. He didn't know how these two had been caught in this place, but Master Tackachul must have used his spirit beast magic to defeat the enemy and been trapped or killed in the process. Barely trained, all Apprentice Matcha could do was wait for help.

"If they're trapped, why was there a banner with the Sanzan symbol on it?" Qing demanded. "Are there any from the sect still in the city?"

"The damned banners are everywhere because the people who live here - accidental refugees, the clan we came in with, and even the beast spirits - think it's a pretty design. Which, to be fair, it is." Apprentice Matcha considered the question a bit longer, then added, "Maybe some Zan Jing'ling are hiding down here, but they'd have to work at it. Have you noticed what the people in here look like?"

"I've never seen people quite like them, actually. They resemble nomads, but...." Master Zhi's voice trailed off. Then, "That old man said there've been people coming in for decades. Nomads. Travelers. All getting caught in whatever trap it was your master found. And I'll bet there's some animal spirits among them, too."

"Oh, auntie's figured it out! That's right. They've been interbreeding with the outsiders for decades now, despite the Zan Jing'ling's best efforts."

"Do not call me auntie in that tone, child." Master Zhi scoffed, then focused. "Much as I'd enjoy continuing our usual competition, Matcha, it's high time we figured this out. Tell us what happened and where your master's Warehouse is, then. Every piece of information may be vital."

Without hesitation, having clearly rehearsed her answer for years, Apprentice Matcha set to talking. "The whole thing started when Master Tackachul learned of a hidden cache of books from the old Sanzan sect up in that mountain shrine. I'm sure you saw it."

"We did."

"Well, we looked for it. Found the entrance using the old sect's keywords and brought the books out to be taken home. Except Master Tackachul insisted on examining our find that same night, while we were camping at Hala Lake with one of the local clans."

Master Zhi scoffed, rolling her eyes. "Let me guess. He refused to follow the rules and bring books of uncertain provenance straight back home."

"I tried to remind him what happened the last time. He said this was different. That Sanzan was a great and noble sect when those books were written and there wouldn't be any danger. Except one of the things he found was a glass orb, full of water and a little itty-bitty city. It turned out to be a mustard seed."

Both Qing and Master Zhi stared, aghast. "He... opened... a mustard seed?" Such things were a barely understood form of dimensional magic from several thousand years ago. Some said they were created by Gods, similar to the Wall that protected Khaitan from the Chaos surrounding it. Not even Warehouses could compare with a functioning mustard seed.

"A small mustard seed, I'll grant, but, yes." Ruefully, Apprentice Matcha gestured around them. "He dropped the orb and when it shattered, it opened out into our world. Unfortunately, it was protected by condensed pure-water."

Which, in turn, had flooded the area and blown open the chasm. "So the mustard seed expanded, the city enlarged and was covered by the lake. And from the sound of it, it had a time-shrink effect that reversed when the orb broke."

"I didn't know about that last, but the rest is right. We were lucky. We all ended up inside the city and protected by the shield. But we, and the tribe we were staying with, were stuck."

"At which point you ran afoul of the Zan Jing'ling sect?" Master Zhi asked. "Given their fondness for storing spirit folk, I can't imagine they'd leave your master alone, him being an octopus and all."

"He realized they meant to capture him fairly quickly. They'd have loved to collect you, too, Qingqing."

Qing ignored Apprentice Matcha's over-familiarity. "You said he helped the beast spirits beat them?"

"It took every weapon we had in our Warehouse and all the spirit beasts and commoner slaves in the pagoda, but, yes. As far as I can tell, he and the others emptied the city of the lot." Apprentice Matcha managed a smile. "I'm not sure, but I think he turned the pagoda's tower into a repelling trap."

A thought occurred to Qing. "How do you eat?" Water wouldn't be a problem, or shouldn't be, given they were under a lake, but food must surely be harder.

"The pagoda used to be the spirit beast compound. There's a whole hunting ground in there, complete with all the sheep and horses and oxen the Wolf Clan owned. Not to mention a decent population of normal animals. Oh, and I taught the clansmen to garden, so we have fruits and vegetables."

Wait. That meant the pagoda was a sub-dimension inside this one? Whomever it was created the place had to have been practically a God. Qing shook his head. "We need to fetch your Warehouse, but if it's holding the enemy off...."

"I'm not sure it is anymore. I haven't seen much motion out there for a year or so now."

Qing turned to Master Zhi. "The pagoda sticks out of the dome. I'm willing to wager the Warehouse is at the top. It might be for the best if I swam to it."

She patted him on the head. "How many times do I have to tell you that I don't send children to do an adult's work? If we go, we go together."

To be honest, Qing didn't object at all.

修炼

Lacking weapons, Apprentice Matcha remained inside the city once she'd shown them to the gate. "This is the safest path. The ink doesn't come down this far."

"Are there any dangers we should be aware of?" Master Zhi asked.

"The few water-born spirit beasts we have won't go more than twenty feet outside the wall. That ink up there scares them. So maybe? Maybe not. Depends on if there's any Zan Jing'ling disciples still out there. It's not like I can check, after all."

That being unarguable, Qing and his master entered the water, using a dozen night-pearls to light their way. It barely helped once they swam up into the inky darkness. A single night-pearl could usually illuminate a room comfortably, but even this many weren't enough. It was like shining a string of lanterns on dense fog.

What little they could see made matters worse. They hadn't been able to tell what lurked nearby earlier, hadn't been able to see what kept brushing up against Qing. Now he knew what they were.

There were bodies in the water. Dozens upon dozens of waterlogged bodies that kept bumping and bumping and bumping into him. At first, he thought the current was pushing them, then he remembered how still this lake was and realized the bodies were moving on their own.

They were ugly things. Bloated. Long hair trailing, reaching, as if alive. Eyes wide, covered with a white film. Their fingers were tipped with claws as long as an old scholar's, stretching out towards Qing and Master Zhi as if to rip them apart.

They couldn't touch Master Zhi. The same thing that'd protected them earlier protected them now. A Book Hunter's clothes were embroidered with arrays, guarding against dozens of different types of attack. As for Qing, well his hide was thick and tough, covered in hardened scales. They could strike but they could not harm.

The danger lay in their numbers. There were far too many of them for Qing and Master Zhi to push through. Every time Qing twisted sideways the undead shifted position.

"They're herding me...."

"I did notice. Keep trying to push back. Find any weak point and use it."

Qing obeyed, though he kept slipping further and further from his target. It didn't make sense. Undead shouldn't have enough intelligence to herd their prey. Shouldn't have the cunning to trick them into a trap. Yet these undead were definitely herding him and if there wasn't a trap at the end of the only path he could find, he'd eat a bare hook. He slowed, lashing with his tail to keep the undead behind him from getting too close. "Something's wrong."

"And what do you do when something seems off?"

The answer was to stop and examine the surroundings if possible. If not, you looked for escape and took it fast. These undead were slow, their actions making it seem like everything was coincidence. Qing slowed more, peering through the murky waters.

A moment later he could have kicked himself if he had feet. Sometimes he got so used to being human he forgot how to be a fish. He'd even used his abilities coming down this way. He'd have to meditate on the subject of using one's assets to the fullest later.

He let his whiskers float out around him, feeling along the bodies and searching for a clue. It was risky. His whiskers were more sensitive than his hide and the bodies could have harmed him if they only knew it. But while they behaved intelligently when it came to herding their victims, they didn't recognize a weak point.

His whiskers slid along the closest body, seemingly unfelt. A perfectly normal drowned corpse, or so it seemed. When he reached the feet, impossible to see due to the ink, he gasped. "Tentacle," he told Master Zhi. "Master Tackachul?"

She took his meaning quickly. Master Tackachul was probably the only one around with long boneless arms. Qing would have asked why their ally would be trying to harm them but this wasn't the time. He headed where the bodies were thickest, slamming through them, breaking past, and almost dropping through the city's dome again.

This time he swooped upwards, evading both attack and yet another long fall. "What should we do?"

Master Zhi released his mane. "I'll handle Brother Tackachul if it is him. You get to that Warehouse and stay with it."

Stay with it? Not deactivate? "But...."

"If Brother Tackachul is an enemy, the Warehouse may be all that's keeping the city safe from his tools. If he's confused, he might still attack. Now go!"

Accepting his orders, Qing spun around in the water and raced towards the pagoda's spire. Or at least he hoped he was racing towards the spire. In this inky blackness, it was impossible to tell.

As he rushed, he slammed into the chasm walls three times and came close to dropping through the city's protective dome twice. Couldn't they have made that dome solid, so no poor fish would wind up crashing through? Couldn't they?

Those near misses with the dome proved invaluable, however. Each time he caught sight of the city below and reoriented towards the center. Until at last, he found his way to the pagoda rising up above the dome into the darkness. Immediately, Qing squirmed along the edges of the pagoda, finding his way to the top level and the spire. He paused, glaring furiously. Warehouse? There was supposed to be a Warehouse here? A Warehouse in defense mode? Nothing of the sort. The only thing there was the spire itself, with a banner drooping at its tip.

A Warehouse in defense mode should be a glowing sphere marked with an array pattern, its energies clearly visible. The only sphere here was the gold ball the spire stuck out of. That was part of the pagoda, surely, not the Warehouse.

Qing nosed the thing. Nosed around the spire. Felt around with his whiskers and suddenly tasted a familiar flavor near the banner. Sandalwood, the most favored material used to create a Warehouse. But the banner was cloth, drooping and folded in on itself.

He nosed the banner. Pushed it around. Nabbed a corner with his lips. Pulled it tight. There! There was the Warehouse, defense array ready but not set. Qing didn't know what'd happened here, nor why the Zan Jing'ling hadn't broken into the City with the defense array in this state. It didn't matter because it was obvious what he had to do.

He shifted to human, grasping the spire with one hand, tracing the array with the other. He couldn't set a strong defense, young and weak as he was. Anything was better than nothing, though, especially now.

To his delight, his *qi* proved stronger than he expected. Energy flared around and through the array. A globe of pale blue light, flickering with his lightning, spread out from the spire, growing rapidly.

It pushed the inky shadows away. Pushed the bodies back. Slid past Master Zhi where she floated, a dozen yards away, tying an octopus' arms into an elaborate knot: Double Happiness, Qing thought.

Master Zhi's voice was faint, coming through the water, but Qing made it out easily and almost burst with pride as she called, "Adequately done. Now help me drag Brother Tackachul back into the city so we can have a nice, long, chat."

修炼

"You absolute idiot."

Master Tackachul sat sulkily in the grass, glared at by both Master Zhi and Apprentice Matcha. Meanwhile, Qing devoured stacks and stacks of steamed breads and grilled meats. He was ravenous, thanks to his newly increased *qi* strength. The only thing he wanted to think about was eating.

They were still inside the city, having gone to the pagoda's hunting grounds to discuss what'd happened and what their next move would be. Not that there were many choices. They couldn't leave this place unguarded. Another outsider might stumble on it and cause trouble. They'd have to get it to Khaitan somehow.

"I didn't think it was a mustard seed," Master Tackachul complained. "I've worked with them before and the thing just looked like a globe with another globe and a model city inside."

Really, he'd been lucky the inner globe hadn't broken and flooded the city. Doubly lucky he'd gotten all the clansmen safely inside. And triply lucky he'd realized the danger from the Zan Jing'ling.

Master Zhi sighed. "It's not just you breaking a mustard seed dimension open. It's you getting yourself so caught up fighting your enemies you lost track of how to be a person."

That was a problem Spirit Beasts had. Even if they cultivated themselves to humanity, they could easily revert to their animal instincts. Master Tackachul had fought the Zan Jing'ling so hard he'd forgotten the difference between friend and foe. It was only when his Warehouse's defenses were activated that he'd regained his self-awareness.

Master Tackachul pouted. "I didn't mean to. And you didn't need to tie me in a knot to stop me. I was waking up. It was only a week or so...."

"It was only a week or so to you. That time shift meant you didn't know how long Apprentice Matcha was waiting for you. It's been ten years inside the city and she's gone and grown too old to be an apprentice anymore."

Master Tackachul looked guiltily at Apprentice Matcha. "I'm sorry."

"You should be. I've been stuck taking care of the mess you left behind for me." Apprentice Matcha sniffed. "You're just lucky I'm enjoying myself."

"Oh, well. That's good."

Master Zhi sniffed. "Not good enough. You're responsible for your apprentice, whether or not she enjoyed herself."

"Oh. I...."

"I even have a husband and a daughter," Apprentice Matcha continued, ignoring the argument. "I might... might... allow her to join the Book Hunters. When she's old enough, that is."

Meekly, Master Tackachul said, "But not as my apprentice?"

She punched him lightly in the shoulder. "Of course as your apprentice. It's not like you're a bad Book Hunter. No one could have predicted that globe held a whole city."

As Master Tackachul sniffled with raw emotion Master Zhi said, "Repairing the globe shouldn't be too difficult with two Hunters and two Warehouses full of equipment. Getting it to Khaitan, however, will be your job, Younger Brother. Qing and I have no time to go home just because you were clumsy."

"Mean Elder sister!" Master Tackachul protested. He didn't sound truly upset, however. Likely he didn't want to travel to Khaitan in the company of two bullies instead of one. Small blame to him. Aunt and niece alike had razor-honed tongues.

"There's one thing I'm wondering." At the two Masters' curious expressions, Qing gestured. "The history books say the Zan Jing'ling collected all kinds of spirits. The men's side captured animal spirits, the women, plants. But I only see animals here. Where did the plants go?"

"A good question, Qing," Master Zhi agreed. "But the only ones who know the truth are dead. I doubt we'll find an answer here. Nor are our leadership likely to care."

Which, Qing admitted, was likely true. Zang Shanghu had no particular need to reconnect with the old sects. Not when they had plenty of their own work to do.

Chapter 3: A Mine Full of Trouble

Zhi Wenku paced calmly alongside the river as her apprentice swam up the rapids. "Don't go straight into the strongest current," she reminded him. Really, were all children like this? Thank the Gods she'd never found a reason to raise any of her own. No reason to marry, for that matter. Not anymore.

She shoved that thought away quickly, pausing to watch young Qing roll backward down slippery rocks, silver and blue scales glittering, twisting, and squirming as he fell. He landed in a pool and transformed into his human shape, clinging to the rocks in a dramatic pose of exhaustion.

"Really. Millions of carp make it up rivers to spawn every year and here you are, bigger than your kinsfolk and far more intelligent, but you can't manage one measly rapid." She shook her head. "How do you expect to get over the Dragon Gate like that?"

He sniffled, rubbing his forearm across his face. "I'm sorry, Master. The water tasted funny and I let myself get distracted."

The water tasted funny? Young Qing could be a complete over-active nuisance but he didn't lie and he did know water far better than Zhi Wenku did. "Funny how?"

"I don't know. Bitter. Metallic, but not metal."

Qing climbed out of the water and dressed. He could transform his possessions when necessary, but that took extra energy he needed for practicing swimming up the falls. As he did so, she noted a long scratch on his flank, half-hidden by the gorgeous blue and silver markings dappling his skin.

"Didn't I tell you to stop if you hurt yourself? And to say something?"

"Oh, that? It's nothing."

It was not nothing, especially if there was something in the water that shouldn't be. "Lie down."

"But Master...."

"Down. Now."

He obeyed unwillingly. He often felt it beneath his dignity to acknowledge injuries. Back when he'd been Prince Suzhi's pet, he'd had the constant care and attention of the best healers. When he'd left home to cultivate, however, he'd been desperate to prove he wasn't the coddled and overprotected pet he'd appeared.

"It's not too bad," Zhi Wenku concluded, once she'd bandaged the injury. "As long as whatever you tasted in the water isn't harmful, you should be all right. Speaking of which...."

"I really don't know what the stuff is, but it can't be too dangerous. There's Lian Village up the way. Maybe someone was rude and dumped their garbage in?"

Small villages like Lian did, sometimes, forget their manners. But there was a larger village, Qingshui, just a half-mile down from Lian, one with a great deal more money and influence. If someone in Lian were foolish enough to dump something dangerous into the river there'd be repercussions they couldn't afford.

Well, whatever it was, it didn't seem to have harmed her apprentice. She'd keep an eye on him, just in case, but right that moment there wasn't much else she could do. "We'll keep an ear out, then. Come along. No point in continuing your exercises now. We're getting too close to the village; don't want to be noticed."

Making sure his carp pattern was properly covered, aside from the delicate tracery of lines along his neck and temples, Qing slung their Warehouse onto his back and picked up their bookseller banner. "Any time you're ready, Master."

With that, they continued up the road.

修炼

Lian Village was barely large enough for the little teahouse at its edge. A single-room building, its few tables had seen much better days. But the tea they served was fresh and hot and the smell of steamed chicken carried the refreshing scent of ginger and garlic.

"We've a well; nice and deep and safe," the old man serving them said. "No need to worry about the river water."

Zhi Wenku blinked, suddenly worried again. "Is there a problem with the river?"

"Oh. You haven't heard? You don't want to be drinking from the river right now. Ain't at all healthy."

That confirmed their suspicion that there was something in the water. Zhi Wenku glanced at Qing, whose wide dark eyes had their usual bemused expression. He really was bright but he had a talent for making himself look a complete fool. Sometimes they needed it.

"I see," she said and added disinterestedly, "We'll take note of that."

"You should. You from Chang'an, then?" The last was asked with an odd sort of interest.

Unsure what was happening, Zhi Wenku agreed. "We were a week or so back. Booksellers like us travel all over the place."

He smiled conspiratorially, "I'm understanding just what you mean, Ma'am. Traveling booksellin's a good way to get around and get to know things, ain't it?"

The old man's manner made Zhi Wenku suspicious. Had he mistaken her for another, expected, guest? Best disabuse him of the notion. "My apprentice and I are interested in scrolls and books. You wouldn't happen to know of anything of that sort?"

The old man frowned, clearly puzzled. "Well now, most of our folk mine the hill up that way, or farm or sew or...." He shrugged. "We're not really much on reading here. Mayor's son's studying to take the provincial test, though. He might, maybe, have something. You should go see him right quick. He's put a fair number of coins into his studies."

Now Zhi Wenku was sure the old man had mistaken her for another. She hoped the actual person showed up soon. The last thing she needed was to get caught up in a local situation. Not, of course, unless it involved books.

Seeing she'd no more questions, the teahouse keeper hesitated, then hastily added, "It all started when them in the mine got stuck. We had to be digging them out from another tunnel; the old one that played out a while back."

It appeared the old man wouldn't be satisfied until he'd told her everything about a case she wasn't involved in. With a sigh, Zhi Wenku said, "You really don't have to tell me all this."

Undeterred, he continued, "We saved 'em, but something cracked in the far back of the old shaft. Whole thing broke apart and poured somethin' in the stream. Mayor's son thought there's something poison in there but Mister Ling didn't like th' idea. We closed up that shaft right quick, but there's still something getting in the water. Nasty. People get real hungry but they can't keep food down, no matter how hungered they are. They eat and they eat and they eat, but it always comes right back. Already had five people die. Only thing saves 'em is if they're stopped from eating. Gotta tie 'em down or keep 'em asleep."

Zhi Wenku couldn't help asking, "And what of Qingshui Village? Have you warned them?"

"Mister Ling, what owns Changshan Mine, went straight down. Last I heard, it ain't hurtin' them. Don't know why. Mayor's son thinks it's di-lu-ted or some such. That means it's weaker, like if I poured water into your teacup now it's half empty."

The mayor's son was probably right. Even so, "You obviously need help, then. I hope...." She was about to say she hoped someone would come soon, but she noticed young Qing had just devoured all the chicken on the plate and grabbed the rice bowl with a determined expression.

"Disciple, where are your manners?"

"Sorry... Master. Can't help it. Hungry!"

The old man stared. "He... did he drink from the river, ma'am? We warned you not to drink from the river!"

She closed her eyes, trying to keep her patience. "No. You didn't. Because we aren't the ones you think we are. If we were the ones you think we are, we wouldn't be pretending to be booksellers. We'd be telling you who we are so we can do something about this."

"But... but... but...."

As Qing reached for Zhi Wenku's rice bowl, she struck his sleep pressure point. He slumped, muttering about how starved he was, while she told the old man, "If nothing else, you need to have someone downriver warning travelers. Gods know how many have drunk from that water already."

"A good half-dozen, possibly more, I'd say." The answer came from the doorway. Zhi Wenku looked to see a tall man in dark traveling clothes, a taller and broader-shouldered boy behind him carrying a book-seller's pack on his shoulders. "At a guess, there's been one of those amusing errors of identification here. I am Shen Wei. This wolf-cub behind me is Xinglu. And I believe I'm the one your village is waiting for, sir."

修炼

While Shen Wei watched, Zhi Wenku slipped a healing pill into young Qing's mouth. "This is a general panacea. Unless the cause is something particularly insidious, it should be enough to cure the problem." She sat back, pulling a coverlet over the boy's body, brushing his hair from his eyes.

Shen Wei eyed her banner. "Zhi Wenku. Your reputation, and that of the Zang Shanghu, precedes you."

Turning her gaze on his banner, seeing only the words 'Shen Wei, Book Seller', she said, "Yours, on the other hand, does not." She stopped him from answering, "I don't actually need to know who you are. My involvement is entirely coincidental and I have no intention of interfering with your business."

A slight smile, half-hidden behind a fan painted with bamboo, "A commendable position." The image on the fan changed. Became the words 'Soul Protection Society'. Changed back. "Especially given Khaitan's agreement with my compatriots."

The Soul Protection Society was a secret group that protected the Tang Kingdom from supernatural threats. Khaitan, being a separate and hidden kingdom, had long since formed a treaty with them. Neither was allowed to interfere in the others' business unless asked.

"Indeed," Zhi Wenku told him. "As far as I know, there's nothing here to interest me... except, of course, making sure my apprentice is all right."

"An understandable desire." The fan lowered and Shen Wei turned serious. "Far be it for me to demand help. But given you're here and given you and your fellow collectors have access to potentially useful tools, materials, and knowledge, I'd appreciate it if you did. The Soul Protection Society has never come across this particular difficulty before."

She stroked Qing's damp forehead. "I said that panacea will cure most simple problems. This may not qualify. I'll help as much as I can. Please remember that I am not the sort of cultivator that chases monsters or battles demons. If such appear, I shall be leaving that to you and your apprentice."

The smile broadened. "Of course. Speaking of whom, shall I leave Xinglu to keep an eye on your apprentice while we talk with the one who sent for me: the mayor's son, young Cui Wen?"

"Frankly, the only thing I'd like better is my apprentice fully recovered."

修炼

Walking through the village Zhi Wenku noted several houses with white hangings covering the entrances. "At least five deaths in the village so far. Did they say how long it took?"

"Young Master Cui's letter said about a week. Between that and your panacea, your apprentice should be safe for the moment."

"You mentioned other victims? Travelers?"

"Mn. Yes." A distant look crossed Shen Wei's face, hard and a little angry. "Young Master Cui's letter said the mine's owner paid for Qingshui Village's mayor's silence, which is why no one put up warnings not to drink the water. I presume your apprentice was thirsty?"

"He's always thirsty." Not knowing Shen Wei well enough, Zhi Wenku didn't say more. Qing's true nature wouldn't matter in Khaitan. Out of

" YOU MENTIONED OTHER VICTIMS. TRAVELERS ? "

their homeland, in places that either didn't believe in spiritual beasts or hunted them? That was a different story altogether. "I presume the owner feared someone would demand recompense?"

"That would be my guess as well," Shen Wei admitted. "From what I understand, the mine is quite lucrative, and he has a monopoly on all copper in the area."

It wouldn't be silver or gold, of course. Such mines were run by the government and Gods help the poor fool who tried to sneakily dig up either metal for themselves. Still, copper was valuable. Mister Ling must have made a pretty fortune.

"Do you know anything more?"

"Young Master Cui sent a sample of the substance that spilled from the mine. I haven't identified it yet, but I'm almost certain some of it comes from a living creature." At her raised brow, he added, "I'm actually an alchemist, not a bookseller. Young Master Cui insisted on this disguise. Said Mister Ling might be suspicious if he knew where I'd come from."

They'd arrived at the largest house in the village by this time. Well, large for varying definitions of large. A mayor's family rated better lodgings than most, but Lian Village only boasted a few dozen families. Mister Ling likely owned something a great deal more elaborate, but his mansion wasn't visible from the village.

The servant who greeted them had expected Shen Wei. He gave Zhi Wenku and her banner an odd look but accepted Shen Wei's assurances that she was his assistant and led them both inside. "Young Master Cui is waiting for you. I will bring you to him immediately."

Following behind silently, Zhi Wenku observed the household furnishings. Plain. Simple. Unassuming. From the looks of things, the mayor had enough integrity to run the village properly. Given his son had sent for help despite Mister Ling's desires, it seemed Cui Wen did too.

A soft knock on the study door was answered by a faintly distracted "Enter." To Zhi Wenku's surprise, the servant didn't obey immediately. Instead, he listened carefully, only sliding the door open when he was satisfied by some faint click.

The room beyond was the oddest study Zhi Wenku had ever seen. Most scholars contented themselves with books upon books and Cui Wen had those too. What she hadn't expected were the scores of odd devices and tools that filled the shelves as well.

There was no sign of Cui Wen or seemed not to be, but the servant simply guided the two of them inside, saying, "Young Master Cui, these are the... booksellers... you sent for."

"Two? I didn't think the problem was that big." The answer came from above them and both Zhi Wenku and Shen Wei looked up, where an elaborate-looking wheelchair hung upside-down, clinging to a rail curving around the ceiling. And, strapped into that wheelchair, was a young man not much older than Xinglu.

Spinning the chair along the rail, the boy brought it back down. When he halted in front of them he shifted a lever in his chair, raising his body to an upright position so he could cup gloved hands and bow to them properly. He smiled as he did so, saying, "Greet you both. I am Cui Wen and I do hope you can help us."

Cui Wen was small and lightly built, with a somewhat nearsighted gaze and a pair of lenses perched on his nose. He would have looked the studious scholar but for his messy hair and unkempt robes. Of course, he had been upside down, just a few minutes earlier.

Once introductions were finished, it took a few minutes for the servant to find seats for Zhi Wenku and Shen Wei, a task he did with a much put-upon air. "I shall fetch tea immediately, Young Master Cui," he added as soon as he was done.

"Eh? No need. The tea service is already hot." Cui Wen gestured at an odd device against the wall of the room: a brass cylinder with a dragon carved around it, steam rising from the carving's nostrils. A touch on its head released a stream of dark brown liquid. "Serve them, then run along, would you?"

Accepting the tea, Zhi Wenku waited for the servant to leave, while Cui Wen shifted his chair over to his desk, pulling off tool-tipped gloves as he did so. Within moments he was going through his notes in a distracted sort of way, pausing once in a while to write something on a scrap paper. Only when Shen Wei coughed gently, drawing the young man's attention, did he return to the table and smile ruefully. "Sorry. So much to do."

"So it would seem. You're the one Mechanist Li has been corresponding with, then?" Shen Wei asked.

Realizing these two were off track, Zhi Wenku interrupted. "Fascinating though the subject is, my apprentice has been poisoned by whatever happened to your water and I'd like to be looking for answers, not discussing non-essential business."

The two men glanced at each other ruefully and Zhi Wenku guessed Shen Wei was another who could easily lose himself in curiosities. He controlled the urge, however, adding, "Some of what you sent me came from a living creature. I'm going to need to find the source to do much more about it."

Cui Wen put a map on the table, showing the mountain road leading further up the valley. He pointed at various landmarks: Qingshui Village, Lian Village, and Changshan Mountain. "The mine is here. You've been told the circumstances? About how we rescued some miners and opened something dangerous up in the process?" At Zhi Wenku's agreement, Cui Wen tapped two spots on the map. "The old shaft, the one that played out, is here. The other shaft opened just last year. I'm certain the poison came from the old shaft."

"Has anyone been in there since?"

"I don't think so." Cui Wen frowned at the map. "Mister Ling locked it shut. Forbad anyone from going near. Said it was dangerous. Which it probably was, but...."

"Do you have a map?"

"I'm not supposed to."

Shen Wei fanned himself, gazing amusedly over the delicate paper. "And your point?"

Embarrassed, Cui Wen admitted, "I'll get them. They aren't complete, though. The main shaft goes straight in, with a half dozen side shafts."

"Mostly I'd like to know where the rescue party's shaft started." Shen Wei stopped the boy before he could object. "Before you say it isn't safe, I'd point out that if the source of the poison is inside the mine, someone has to go inside."

Cui Wen sighed. "Yes. I know. And I'll help you. But you're going to have to get past the guards first. Mister Ling has the place shut tight. He had the shaft gated just as soon as it played out. There's no easy way in."

Exactly what Zhi Wenku had expected. "It's still our best chance. No matter how dangerous."

Cui Wen could do nothing but agree with the plan.

修炼

They waited until well past dark before all three headed up the narrow trail towards the copper mine. To Zhi Wenku's surprise, Cui Wen's wheeled chair had been designed to handle rough areas, allowing him to join them despite her better judgment. It even had lights, tiny luminous night pearls embedded in the chair's frame, just bright enough to illuminate the path ahead.

As they went, Shen Wei ordered, "You will remain outside when we get there. We have no idea what to expect."

"I promise I will. I know my limitations." He looked at Zhi Wenku, apparently assuming a book-seller had more access to information than an alchemist, "Do you have any thoughts on what it might be?"

Zhi Wenku thought about it. "I can't think of anything in my bestiary whose poison causes similar symptoms. Possibly my people haven't encountered it."

"It isn't anything I've heard of either." Shen Wei added. "We're pretty much going in blind here."

Cui Wen sighed. "I'm sorry I can't be more help." It was obvious he wanted to be involved and useful. Equally obvious he understood he couldn't. He gestured at his legs, "I've done my best to make up for my lack, but...."

"I think you should consider applying to be Mechanist Li's apprentice. She's getting on in years and you're obviously equally talented."

"My father says maybe when I'm older." The boy stopped, pointing up the trail at a shadowy figure leaning against a tree stump. "That's one of the guards," he whispered. "He won't let anyone in. None of them will."

"I'll deal with him," Shen Wei murmured, fading away. Flash-step, a skill most cultivators learned early, but seldom as well. A moment later there was the faintest of sounds as the guard dropped to the ground and Shen Wei returned. "There's five or so more men just outside the shaft and someone in a shack doing paperwork. Knocking them out might draw attention. Any thoughts on a distraction?"

Zhi Wenku took several sheets of paper from her storage scroll. "My turn." She sat on the ground, folding them into a small pack of wolves and setting off the spell with a wisp of *qi*. As they transformed and rushed up the trail, she told her companions, "They're only paper, so they won't last long. But that should be enough."

As startled and frightened shouts rose ahead of them, Shen Wei murmured, "Yes, I think they will."

修炼

If the mine belonged to the government, getting rid of the guards would have been difficult. These men weren't soldiers, however, just big, burly types unused to being chased by wolves. When those wolves couldn't be hurt by arrow or saber, the guards rushed off quickly.

This led to the man in the shack coming out and yelling angrily, only to leap back inside at the sight of the wolves. The shack door slammed shut barely in time to keep the lead paper wolf from snapping at him.

"That was Mister Ling," Cui Wen muttered. "What's he doing here so late at night?"

"A good question. One we should investigate."

Ordinarily, Zhi Wenku would focus on the matter at hand. They'd chased away the guards and needed to enter the mine. If the man in the shack had just been a clerk, busily accounting for the day's business, she'd disagree. Mister Ling, however, might have important information.

They headed for the shack, Zhi Wenku summoning her paper wolves and restoring them to their true form. She'd only lost one, she noted approvingly. The life spell was expensive to prepare and she only had a few dozen sheets left.

Shen Wei waved his fan at the door as they approached, knocking it open with a sharp *bang*. Another crash followed as the man inside fell back against his desk, staring wildly at them as they entered. "Who... who... who..." His eyes fell on Cui Wen and his lips curled back in a snarl. "YOU! What are you doing here?"

Cui Wen tilted his head inquiringly. "Mister Ling, I'm just helping some friends."

"I told your father you'd be trouble when he adopted you! If you don't stop interfering...."

"Father may be under your thumb, Mister Ling. I'm not." Cui Wen moved sideways, gesturing at Shen Wei. "This is your business, though. Please, Master Shen."

Shen Wei glanced sharply at the boy. "I'm not here to be your weapon."

"You're not a weapon, or a tool, sir. I promise. But Mister Ling has been up to something for years now. It's high time someone took note of it."

Guessing Cui Wen was one of those idealist scholars who tried to speak up against perceived corruption and unrighteousness, or at least wanted to be, Zhi Wenku didn't bother arguing. "Mister Ling. What, exactly, is in your mine?"

A sneer. "Why should I answer anything you say, bookseller?" At Zhi Wenku's raised brow, he added, "Yes. I know you're some wandering bookseller whose apprentice just made himself ill, drinking the river water."

"You have a spy, I see. Did they mention Mister Shen here at all?"

Scoffing, Mister Ling waved a derogatory hand at Shen Wei. "Another bookseller. Another apprentice. Nothing important. I don't know why you've brought them, Cui Wen. Or are you going to pretend they're government agents, come to see if you're right about my criminal activities? You think I haven't handled that problem?"

Cui Wen looked ready to leap out of his chair and smash the man in the mouth. "Your extra wealth comes from somewhere," he snarled. It wasn't a pretty look on that young face. "It isn't doing a damned thing to help your people."

All of this was very interesting but not getting them anywhere. Zhi Wenku glanced inquiringly at Shen Wei and at his slight smile of agreement, stepped between the pair. "I'm not a government agent," she said quietly, voice low but dangerous. "I am, however, out of patience. Answer my question, Mister Ling."

Zhi Wenku was skilled at getting cooperation from the uncooperative; a talent practiced over years and years of dealing with stubborn compatriots, stubborn writers, and even more stubborn books. She gazed quietly into the man's eyes, making it clear she'd brook no further argument.

"I don't know what it is. Master Lao said it would pass soon. Once it's dilute enough there won't be a problem."

"Master Lao? Who is this Master Lao?"

A shrug. "A sorcerer. He's been helping increase the mine's output."

That wasn't the sort of thing sorcerers usually did. "How is he doing this? And what is the 'it' that's supposed to go away soon?"

The mine owner spread his hands helplessly. "I hired him find out why our old shaft played out sooner than expected. It was like someone took the... metal... out before we could get to it. He almost recovered everything lost, but it needs a special method to extract."

Interesting. Zhi Wenku was about to ask more but Cui Wen suddenly spoke up. "There's more to it than that." He wheeled over to Mister Ling's desk and pointed at the two open account books. "This is his real account. He's copying part of it into the other."

Both Zhi Wenku and Shen Wei looked at the pages, spotting the difference right away. There was a symbol on one book that didn't appear on the other. Shen Wei pointed at it. "I don't recognize this, but perhaps you do, Bookseller Zhi?"

"I don't. But I can try translating it." She slid a lens from the handle of her whisk and held it over the page. Immediately the glass shimmered, showing another character entirely. "Silver?"

Cui Wen turned white. "Silver? Truly? Are you mad?"

Lips tight, Mister Ling refused to answer. He didn't need to. By mining silver without ceding it to the government, he and everyone who worked for him could be arrested. Depending on how much silver was involved, he and his family would be executed. Depending on how much anyone else in the area knew, they might share his fate. At the very least there were prison sentences involved.

Quickly, Cui Wen turned to Shen Wei. "My village doesn't know anything about this. Even our miners... I swear...."

Shen Wei stopped him. "The Soul Protection Society's only business is cultivational and sorcerous. We have nothing to do with Imperial law. I won't take this to court." He turned a sharp gaze on Mister Ling. "I do, however, suggest you do what you ought to have done when you discovered the silver vein. Report it to your governor before it's too late."

Mister Ling wilted. "It's already too late," he whimpered. "That's why I hired that sorcerer. He was supposed to get it back. He has been getting it back, but it's already been refined... so I can't just take it to the government."

Zhi Wenku didn't understand. "Explain."

With a sigh, Mister Ling obeyed. "Last year my foreman discovered a vein of silver. He and I dug further in, intending to measure the length, and found it went a good three hundred feet into the mountain. I was going to report it, I swear I was. Except... it started disappearing. The rock just... crumbled where the silver was. It was like something sucked the stuff out. I... I panicked. Some of the men knew about the ore already. I was afraid they'd talk. But how could I explain its disappearance?"

Zhi Wenku suspected Mister Ling would've stolen the silver if he could get away with it. He didn't strike her as particularly ethical. But the stuff disappearing entirely would have been terrifying. "Do you know of anything that can suck silver from its ore like that, Master Shen?"

"It could be a spirit beast of some sort, one with an affinity for treasure: a jin chan or pixiu or even a corrupted dragon. Or perhaps a sorcerer, drawing the stuff out with an array. I'd have to look at it to guess."

If Qing were there, Zhi Wenku would have sent him into their Warehouse to research the question. But he was still unconscious. "I could search for an answer but given our lack of time, I don't think that's a good idea."

Shen Wei agreed. "Our next step is to discuss the matter with this Master Lao. Mister Ling, where can we find him?" He seemed friendly. His expression was not.

Frightened, Mister Ling pointed towards a locked gate some yards away. "He works at night so he won't be disturbed. You'll find him in a chamber at the far end of the third right shaft."

Visualizing the map, Zhi Wenku noted how close the rescue shaft came to that described position. The rescuers must have cracked the stone and opened a way into the sorcerer's hidden study, spilling his experiment into the river.

"Very well. Young Master Cui, you stay with Mister Ling." Zhi Wenku summoned her paper wolves and set them to guard the boy. "They aren't your pets and they won't attack at your order," she warned. Cui Wen might be playing a long game or he might just be stopping Mister Ling from doing more harm. Either way, she didn't want to be responsible if her paper wolves got out of hand because a human child panicked.

"I understand," he said, looking mildly downcast. To his credit, he didn't try to explain or defend himself. "I'll use the time to go over Mister Ling's records, then, shall I?"

"An excellent idea," Shen Wei agreed. "I'd be especially interested in any alchemical products he's ordered. We might have to know that in the near future."

Indeed. If the sorcerer died or escaped before they could get the truth out of him, they'd need some other source of information. And, hopefully, one of them would work out what to do with it.

修炼

The old shaft was barricaded by a large iron gate, locked with a huge iron padlock. The rectangular structure hung from the latch as if to bellow, 'NO. ONE. ENTERS," in the voice of the guardian beast carved into its surface.

"My turn," Zhi Wenku told her companion, flicking her whisk at the padlock, sending strands of kirin hair twisting down into the center. A few careful flicks and the lock fell open, landing on the ground with a crash.

"Nice," Shen Wei murmured. "I've always admired your sect's tools. That translation device of yours, as well."

She shrugged off the compliment. "We have the advantage of more sorcerers and cultivators in Khaitan. More magic and *qi* for that matter."

He smiled ruefully. "You pay a price for that if memory serves. Your sorcerers and cultivators have to work harder to keep it controlled."

That was exactly true. "It's led to some difficult situations in the past.

Will likely lead to difficult situations in the future." The land that was now Khaitan had been changed and warped several times in its history. They could easily be changed again. Such was the price of the power they contained.

They hiked to the far end of a side shaft that appeared to come to a dead end, just as Mister Ling had said. Shen Wei examined the rock for a moment, then the words on his fan changed to talismanic script. A single wave flung those words - gleaming green-gold - to strike the stone wall ahead of them.

The wall dissolved, revealing more tunnel ahead. Dark, with a faint glow in the distance. Something groaned, a peculiar, unhappy noise that reminded her of the time Qing had gotten into a pile of fermented apples. He'd been sick for days.

"That sounds like me, the time I ate too many New Year's dumplings," Shen Wei muttered. At her raised brow, he added ruefully, "I love the stuff. Can't get enough. If Xinglu weren't there to stop me, I could eat a whole cartful."

Zhi Wenku sighed, wondering if she were the only adult in the room. Instead of remarking on the foolishness of gorging on any sort of food, she shook her head and continued up the tunnel.

The chamber at the end of the shaft was large and dim except for a lighted area towards the center. Off to the side, just visible against the wall, was a pool of something dark and noisome, stinking of sickness. A hastily mended retaining wall made it obvious this was the source of whatever contaminated the river.

Movement further inside the chamber drew their attention. A cauldron hung above a fire, simmering away, the stench of bitter herbs and minerals drifting towards Zhi Wenku and Shen Wei. A man stood beside the thing, startlingly tall and thin, with oddly pale hair.

"A Pamir native?" Zhi Wenku whispered, puzzled. "But his hair isn't red enough."

As more groans covered the sound of their speech, Shen Wei disagreed. "More likely a foreign devil. They usually don't come this far, though."

The foreign devils were outlanders who came to these lands via the silk trade. "So a merchant? But what is he doing?"

Right then the man was filling a huge bowl with whatever was in that cauldron. For a moment Zhi Wenku thought he meant to drink it, but instead, he carried it into the shadows, towards the source of that noise. He spoke roughly, sounding annoyed, but his words weren't comprehensible, at least not to Zhi Wenku.

"He wants someone back there to drink," Shen Wei muttered in her ear. "We're going to have to get nearer to find out who."

"Right. How do you want to go about this?"

"You get his attention while I check his captive. At least I'm betting it's a captive. No beast makes noises like that because it's happy."

A sensible idea. Zhi Wenku slid her fingers along the sigils on her whisk, choosing an element as she set it to fighting mode. No flames. Not when they didn't know if there was something flammable. Wind should be enough for the moment.

They both moved quickly, Shen Wei to the side, Zhi Wenku towards the circle of light. Waiting for the sorcerer to return to his cauldron, she crouched in the shadows. If the man looked up he'd notice her immediately. He was too focused on his task to do so.

Zhi Wenku moved, snapping her whisk at the man's back. To her intense annoyance, it missed. Not because she'd aimed poorly but because there was a shield array guarding him. The entire center area of the cave was protected.

The sorcerer dropped his bowl. Cursing, or at least it sounded like a curse, he drew a short stick, heavily carved with symbols similar to the one Zhi Wenku had translated earlier. A blast of fire shot through the air at her. She batted it aside easily with her whisk.

Glaring, they both shifted position, each watching the other and trying to find a better vantage point. Naturally, he stayed inside the circle of his protected area, sending ball after ball of fire racing at her.

His shield wasn't in his favor. Oh, it protected him from attack but it kept him contained. The only way he could deal with Zhi Wenku was to keep moving in a small area, constantly shifting to keep himself facing her.

She pointed at the cauldron, smoking oddly and about ready to boil over. "I don't know if you understand me, but your potion's overheating."

"Shut up!" he snapped in poorly accented Chinese. "Liar!"

Smiling, she snapped her whisk to keep another fireball from striking her. "Hear without listening? Pay the price." She shifted around again, forcing the sorcerer to keep his eyes on her. Things were going to be unpleasant in a moment.

"I'll send you to perdition!" The word he used was unfamiliar but she didn't need to know it to guess his meaning. "You female dog!"

If his attacks were as effective as his defense Zhi Wenku might have worried. As it was, all she could do was keep his attention on her while Shen Wei did something about whatever was making that noise. It'd gone quieter, now, but she couldn't tell why.

The cauldron bubbled and smoked, until the sorcerer finally recognized what was happening. He reacted too late, failing to dodge the liquid boiling over the sides and into the fire. Steam and smoke poured off the flames, enveloping him. His screams choked off to small whimpers as he rolled weakly on the floor.

Smoke spread as the sorcerer's shield failed and Zhi Wenku shouted, "Shen Wei, look out!"

"On it," the cultivator called. "Get back." A moment later he rushed out of the darkness, fan sweeping up and down, driving the smoke and steam into the pool they'd seen earlier. Zhi Wenku used her whisk to guide the smaller wisps in as well, keeping it all from escaping.

It took several minutes for the stuff to clear, at which point she turned to her companion. "Is this the poison? And what the hell was that idiot using it for?"

Shen Wei smiled ruefully. "Come with me," he said, leading her back into the shadowed corner where something huge and fluffy huddled. "She's why the silver vein disappeared."

The gold-furred beast was a pixiu, a spirit beast who could eat vast quantities of treasure. The trick was that once they had, they could never excrete the stuff, only regurgitating it for their owner. No one had tried to force it to give up what they'd consumed. No one but the sorcerer lying sprawled amid the wreckage of his work.

"So the poison was intended to make this poor thing vomit it out?"

"Yes. She tells me he'd force it down her, then filter the treasure from what she'd vomited, storing the waste in that pool."

"And that's what contaminated the river." Not a question. A statement. "Is there a cure?" That was Zhi Wenku's main concern. She had faith in young Qing's ability to survive what a human might not, but she didn't like seeing him suffer.

"That's something we'll have to ask the poison's creator, if he survived." Shen Wei patted the pixiu on the head lightly, telling her to sit quietly and wait. Then he and Zhi Wenku both went back to the sorcerer.

He looked miserable. Covered in ash and stinking of alchemical ingredients. Curled up in a ball, he groaned as loud or louder than the spirit beast he'd been tormenting. "...help..."

Squatting, grasping the man's chin, Zhi Wenku told him, "Help depends on cooperation. Your poison has killed people. Is there a cure?"

"It shouldn't have needed a cure! It barely did anything to that damn treasure eater!" He whined loudly, crying, "I didn't expect it to kill anyone!"

Of course, he didn't. Consequences were what happened to other people, apparently. "Could you come up with a cure, given time?"

"...could... but... Oh God in Heaven... going to be sick!"

"That panacea of yours?" Shen Wei asked softly.

She'd been thinking much the same thing. Drawing the man's attention she told him, "I've a pill to stave off the poison. I doubt it's a permanent cure." A poison strong enough to force a pixiu to vomit up its treasure was quite a bit more than a low-level all-heal could counteract. Even the strongest ones in Khaitan's markets might have trouble with it.

Shen Wei grasped the man's elbow. Pulled him to his feet. "We'll just have to fetch all your notes and see what we can come up with. Good thing I'm an alchemist. This may take a while."

With that, they dragged the sorcerer out of the mine. They had a lot of work to do.

Chapter 4: Unexpected Diversions

"We need you two to take my crane-ship to Khai City and fetch more panacea. In fact, fetch high-grade panacea, because I think we're going to need it."

Qing frowned. Master Zhi's crane-ship was a flying device designed to mimic a crane in flight. One rode in the wooden platform on the thing's back or inside its body if you didn't mind being crowded. It was also damned expensive. Master Zhi seldom allowed him to touch the controls.

Knowing better than to argue, Qing accepted the compass-like device used to pilot the crane. Then realization hit. "Two? You mean you want me to take Xinglu?" Master Shen's apprentice was an outsider. They weren't supposed to bring outsiders into Khaitan.

Master Zhi sniffed. "There's no law against it and I don't want you going on your own. Just because it looks like you're recovering doesn't mean you have. That poison is insidious."

Qing didn't want to think about that damned poison. Didn't want to think about how hungry and how sick he'd been. It had to be horrible for humans, with their weaker constitutions and more fragile spirits. Right now the panacea Master Zhi carried was the only thing helping.

"How much should I get?" Or, rather how much he could spend? Master Zhi was a frugal woman, some might say miserly. To his surprise, she shoved a string of Khaitanese electrum flowers at him. He'd never seen quite so much money before and his jaw gaped unabashedly at the sight. One could buy a village with that much.

Master Shen handed him a solidly packed block of Jade Bamboo tea. "Your Master tells me this is highly valued in Khaitan. Sell it and use the funds as well."

That... was a great deal of money. More money than Qing had ever carried. More money than he'd ever seen spent at once. He reflected quickly on the price of high-grade panacea and realized they'd be needing every blossom. "I'll fetch Xinglu, then."

"No need. My young wolf is waiting with the crane-ship." Shen Wei yawned suddenly, clearly exhausted from several days' effort. "You just get moving. And be careful."

With a quick bow to both Masters, Qing hurried off.

修炼

The crane-ship sat on a flat area just outside of the village, blue-grey wings folded around its body, long beak tucked as if it were asleep. From a distance, it looked like a mere bird, albeit one with a wooden railed platform installed on its back. Only when one drew close did one realize how big it actually was.

Xinglu lounged in the crane-ship's shadow, tossing stones at self-determined targets. Cui Wen waited too, sipping elegantly from a cup of tea. "Ah... come to see us off?" Qing asked, guessing the answer. Cui Wen wore travel clothes with a large pack attached to his chair. Before the boy could correct him, he added, "You can't come."

"I've been telling him that for the last ten minutes," Xinglu grumbled. "He won't leave."

"That's because I have to come. If I stay here, Mister Ling's backer will be after me."

Mister Ling's backer? Qing knew the mine owner had been behind the poison that'd nearly killed him and had killed a good dozen or so others. "What are you talking about?"

"I don't know who he is, but he helped Mister Ling find that sorcerer of his. And Mister Ling was giving him a good sixty percent of the shares."

Qing wasn't much on numbers. "I've no idea what you mean."

"Mister Ling wouldn't give away over half the silver he stole for no reason. He especially wouldn't risk stealing silver at all without someone more powerful behind him. That's a capital offense for the whole family."

"The whole family? They'd kill everyone just for that? It's just theft, isn't it?" Both Xinglu and Cui Wen eyed him like he'd grown a second head. "What?"

"You're a Book Hunter and you don't have the slightest comprehension of history or politics?"

He sniffed. "Fine. I'm an ignorant fish with no understanding of the world around me. Would you please explain?"

Cui Wen did so, "Any mine owner who produces silver or gold tithes ninety-five percent to the Emperor. Copper can be sold at market price but the government gets first dibs."

He blinked. "Oh. You mean it's like electrum. Or ice jade."

"That's what Khaitan uses, right?" At Qing's agreement, Xinglu told him, "Yes. Exactly."

"But it's still just theft. Would they kill children? Cousins? Brothers and sisters and wives?" Seeing Xinglu and Cui Wen's reaction, Qing felt sick. "That's... disgusting."

"It is," Cui Wen agreed. "It's also the way things are. The point is, Mister Ling has someone behind him. Someone who wouldn't want anyone knowing they're pulling the strings. They'll sacrifice him without a qualm. They'll kill anyone who knows they're out there."

By which Cui Wen meant himself. Qing looked at Xinglu. "I think, maybe, it'd be best if Cui Wen came with us after all."

With a sigh, Xinglu agreed.

修炼

The trip to Khaitan went quietly, as did the purchase of several packs of high-quality panacea. Qing did have to keep a close eye on his companions throughout. They kept trying to wander off and into whatever troubles they could find in the back-street alleys of Khai City.

Still, their task completed, Qing managed to get them back to the crane-ship without too much trouble, a fact Xinglu couldn't help remarking on. "Really, I'd expected at least one or two fights."

"Do you always borrow trouble?" Qing couldn't help asking as they reboarded the crane-ship's platform.

"Oh, no. It finds me without my having to look." A gentle shove got Cui Wen up, then Xinglu bounded atop the platform next to Qing. "You know how it is."

Truthfully, Qing did know, so he didn't pursue the question, just set them flying. At the same time, Cui Wen poked at the wooden feathers covering the crane-ship's body. "I was too busy gawking on the way here to ask. How does this work?"

"I don't know. I'm not a mechanist or a sorcerer." Qing eyed the crane-ship thoughtfully. "Master Zhi keeps it for when we have to get somewhere fast, but we don't use it often."

"Really?" Fascination suffused Cui Wen's features. "I'd ride it all the time. Can you let it fly and sleep down in the hold?" He pointed at the hatch.

"Someone has to keep an eye on its path, so no. And I prefer flying myself over being flown." If he'd been on his own he wouldn't have bothered with this big clunky thing at all.

"You can fly?" Xinglu tilted his head curiously. "I thought you were a fish of some sort?" Xinglu gestured at the scale pattern running along Qing's body. It was too warm to bother with a full robe and Qing had tossed it to the side to cool off.

"Isn't that a tattoo?" Cui Wen asked, clearly confused.

"No. I'm a dragon-carp. Not cultivated enough to leap over the Dragon Gate, of course, but cultivated enough to treat air like water. I almost have legs, too!"

"Is that why you recovered from the poison so fast?" At Qing's agreement, Xinglu explained to Cui Wen, "He's a spirit beast."

"Oh." It was obvious Cui Wen wanted to know more, but something drew his attention. "How big is this crane," he asked, gazing at the mountains below.

"Ah... about ten feet wide and twenty feet long." Qing wondered at the sudden subject shift. "Do you feel cramped? Would you like to go below and rest?"

Cui Wen pointed below them. "No. There's a shadow down there that seems large compared to us."

They peered over the side, finding the crane's shadow flickering against the pale landscape. Further behind and gaining fast was a turtle-shaped shadow several times larger than theirs.

Qing searched for the source of that other shadow. Nothing. The sky seemed pure pale blue and empty, with only a few dozen thin and fluffy clouds scattered across its expanse.

Suspicious, Qing handed the controller to Xinglu. He'd already taught both companions how to use it. Now he was glad he had. "I'm going to

" CAN YOU LET IT FLY AND SLEEP DOWN IN THE HOLD ? "

check it out," he told them, leaping off the crane's back and transforming as he went.

Whatever followed them might be innocent. He wouldn't risk his mission or his friends assuming that.

修炼

The air away from the crane's protection was icy cold. If Qing's scales weren't thicker than any fish born, he'd have been freezing. The wind didn't help, slamming him in all directions as he fought his way through.

Fortunately, he'd been ready for both cold and wind. Gaining his bearings, he scanned the ground for that second shadow, then worked out where the thing casting it had to be. He almost swam right into whatever it was. Hidden behind an invisibility array, all he could tell was that it was carved from dense stone. Given its shadow, there was only one thing it could be.

"But why would someone make a flying turtle?" he asked plaintively. A crane made sense but turtles had nothing to do with the air.

He swam below the object, drawing on his sense of air currents. His cultivation had increased, he noted happily. He might not be able to see the thing with his eyes but the wind defined its shape clearly. Yes. Definitely a turtle. One with a small building atop the shell.

It seemed innocent, but Qing had his doubts. The thing was clearly following the crane-ship and he didn't like that at all. He swam out of its wake, speeding back to the crane. "It's a turtle carved from stone," he told them, settling on the railing, not bothering to change back. "And big."

Xinglu scanned the sky behind them, then the ground below. "I don't like how close it's getting. Is it a puppet like this one?"

"More like a statue. The limbs don't move."

"So it isn't going to try and eat us?"

Given its size, the crane would fit in the damned thing's wide open mouth without needing to bite down. "I wouldn't guarantee that. Any thoughts on how to evade it?"

"Honestly? We're best off abandoning ship... I mean bird... and seeing what it does. Set the crane to fly in a circle until we have a chance to come back for it."

Traveling afoot meant they'd be days getting back to their masters. Worse, they'd have to carry Cui Wen. His chair could do far more than most such tools, but it surely couldn't handle rough forest terrain. Still,

Qing didn't like that turtle. Friendly strangers didn't chase you, hidden behind an invisibility array.

"We can't escape if we stay with the crane," Cui Wen pointed out, looking ruefully at his chair. "We'll have to leave this...."

"No. I have a *qiankun* bag," Xinglu pointed out. "Quickly, then. Let's get away before they catch up."

Relieved that they wouldn't have to argue when they'd no time to do so, Qing grew larger and let Cui Wen sit on his back. At the same time, Xinglu folded the chair up and stuffed it into his bag, then stuck the bag into his sleeve.

"That sort of thing always amazes me," Cui Wen said, clinging to Qing's mane. "Imagine what sort of mechanisms I could create if I could build arrays like that."

Qing thought that sounded fascinating but this wasn't the time to explore the possibilities. Instead, he set the crane flying at its fastest and dove off the side. Xinglu was close behind, leaping onto his black sword in one practiced move.

They dodged downwards into the trees, praying the owner of the turtle didn't notice their escape. Praying, too, that the crane wouldn't crash somewhere. Master Zhi would understand, but she'd still be furious.

修炼

When night fell they found a place to camp, Xinglu setting up a protective array around them and Cui Wen placing warning devices out. "They won't stop anyone from coming in," he noted. "But we'll know they're there if we hear a tree frog singing."

Since tree frogs didn't live this high in the mountains their call could only be from one of the devices. An intelligent intruder might recognize it as a warning. It might even make them back off, though Qing wasn't optimistic.

Setting the crane-ship's control device on a rock at the center of their campsite, Qing said, "It's still in one piece, according to this. As long as the symbol glows, the crane's still working."

"You can't bring it back, though?"

"Not from this distance. I'll fly to it, once I was sure that turtle's gone." Qing eyed the little sphere worriedly. "I hope it doesn't get damaged. Master Zhi got it from her master and she won't be happy if it comes back in several pieces, or not at all."

They didn't cook dinner. Their supplies included preserved meats and bread; safer than filling the air with the scent of cooking food. Smoke alone wouldn't draw attention. Food, on the other hand, would.

More for something to do than anything else, Qing returned to their earlier discussion. "Cui Wen, do you know much about magic? Or cultivation?"

"Not enough to manage either. Father wants me to be a scholar." A wry smile. "He doesn't believe in such things. Says it's all superstitious nonsense. I wish I could have brought him along on this trip."

Xinglu disagreed. "In my experience, those who don't accept such things won't change their minds based on evidence. I've seen people look at wildly powerful magic and be convinced the whole thing was some elaborate fake."

Qing added, "There's a fair number of fake cultivationists, too. Never buy a book on the subject from any random seller. There's one fellow who just loves tricking kids with trash manuals."

That got a scoff from Cui Wen. "When I was little, one tried convincing me I was the chosen one and would be storming the martial world." His lips tightened slightly before his usual bland expression returned. "I couldn't walk from birth, but I was training to build up my cultivation. At least until the so-called martial world ruined my meridians for me."

"I don't understand," Qing admitted. "You said your father didn't believe in that sort of thing."

A dour chuckle. "My father is actually my mother's brother. He adopted me after my parents were killed. It... it's a long story, but my name used to be Zhu Wen." Cui Wen shrugged. "Father's afraid I'll try to seek vengeance against the *jianghu* for what happened to my family. He's not wrong."

The *jianghu* was the term locals used for those who lived and died by a strict code of martial conduct. Or at least they claimed to. From what Qing understood, the people in the *jianghu* feuded and argued and sometimes murdered whole families in their effort to claim power. Khaitan law forbade such behavior and he wondered why it was allowed here.

Not that he expected to understand any sort of explanation.

修炼

Qing had just barely fallen asleep when Xinglu woke him again. "That crane of yours is coming our way."

"Impossible!" There was no way to control the thing without the device

Qing had brought with them. It should have either kept flying in a circle or been destroyed by the one pursuing it.

"Look."

Qing glared at the control device. The glowing dot that marked the crane's location was, indeed, moving back towards the center. "How?"

Cui Wen, woken by the discussion, took in the situation quickly. "Maybe it was swallowed. You said it was big enough, earlier."

"Perhaps. But why bother?"

"You're tracking the crane with that device? Could they track the device with the crane?"

Qing wasn't sure and said so. "It's moving fast, too. I don't think we can get far enough away to escape if they're hunting us."

"I'm not sure we should try." At Qing and Xinglu's raised brows, Cui Wen explained, "Since they captured the crane instead of destroying it, they must have some use for one or more of us. We might be best off letting them catch up and finding out."

Xinglu frowned. "I hope you don't expect them to have some innocent reason to hunt us down this way?"

"No. No, I don't think anything of the sort. But they might try to make us believe it. If one of us can stay out of their hands, they can get help if we need it." He gestured at Qing. "Your beast-form can change size. How small can you be?"

Qing set his fingers about half an inch apart. "This big." That was a tenth his natural size, a fairly tiny carp, unless one included his barbels and the fine mane and tail he'd recently developed.

"Can you hide in that *qiankun* bag of Xinglu's?"

"No," Xinglu answered before Qing could. "He's a living creature. He wouldn't survive in there."

As Qing agreed, Cui Wen suggested, "Then hide elsewhere and follow later?"

The idea was dangerous. So was making a run for it. Gods knew what their pursuit wanted or how much trouble they'd be in if they were captured, but escape seemed unlikely when Cui Wen was crippled and neither Qing nor Xinglu could fly fast enough to evade that turtle.

"All right," Qing agreed. "If you're both willing, I'll try."

He just hoped nothing would go wrong.

修炼

Their pursuit arrived quickly. Whatever hid the turtle from their sight didn't affect shadows, so its presence created a peculiar vision of a bright moon that cast no light. It was as if they were looking at a painting, instead of the real thing.

"I see an outline." Xinglu gazed at the shadow. "It really is huge."

Anything big enough to swallow the crane would have to be. 'Seeing' it through his sense of the wind, Qing told his companions, "Something's coming. Be ready." He hid in Xinglu's hair, pretending to be a particularly fancy bit of jewelry.

Carved stone statues of armored human soldiers dropped down, carrying stone weapons. They landed heavily, driving partway into the dirt. Unfazed, they climbed out of the holes and walked past the guard array into camp.

To Qing's relief, the stone soldiers didn't attack, just surrounded Xinglu and Cui Wen, stone swords drawn and ready. A moment later an old man's voice said, "Good. Very good. You know when you're outmatched."

Cui Wen started. Stared around. "Grandfather? It's you?"

The speaker was Cui Wen's grandfather? Cui Wen didn't seem happy about it. If anything, he sounded scared. Peeping out through Xinglu's hair, Qing saw the young man had gone ice-pale.

The old man didn't show himself. Instead, he chuckled harshly as one of his soldiers turned and turned again. "Where's the little would-be dragon?"

Oh, dear. Their pursuit knew more about Qing than he ought. Was it better to reveal himself or to continue pretending to be a hair-ornament? Neither seemed a good idea, given how much the enemy knew.

"Doesn't it get confusing, using these statues to see through? So many views," Xinglu mocked. He was trying to irritate their enemy, but there was more to it than that. Xinglu had just told them that all those statues served as the old man's eyes.

With dozens of eyes to see through and one mind to handle it, perhaps Qing could slip out of sight. He couldn't help his companions and hoped they understood. If he escaped he could try rescuing them later.

Although not a full dragon yet, Qing could manipulate weather a bit. He imposed his thoughts on the damp grass and dirt surrounding them. The air warmed the chill ground, drawing the water upwards, creating a slowly thickening fog.

Without needing to be told, his friends did their part to distract their enemy: Cui Wen aiming a small crossbow, Xinglu drawing his black sword. "Stay away," Cui Wen growled threateningly.

"Oh, yes. I'm terribly afraid of that pin shooter. These are stone soldiers, boy. You can't harm them with that."

Cui Wen fired, dart striking the nearest stone soldier in the eye. As promised, the thing didn't seem to notice the injury, moving closer without pause. Except a moment later its head shattered as the dart exploded.

"Oh... You're more talented than I realized, child. Your parents taught you well."

"Don't you dare mention my parents, you old bastard! You're why they're dead!"

All of this sounded fascinating, but this wasn't the time for Qing to hang around and listen. He needed to get away. The two boys couldn't escape capture, even with their unexpectedly powerful weapons. If Qing hoped to rescue them he couldn't be taken as well.

The mist thickened and Qing slithered down Xinglu's back. Burying his nose in the ground, he struggled to worm his way in and failed. He needed to dig and that needed legs. Desperately twisting and flopping, he felt his *qi* surge, pushing his abilities a bit further. Short limbs formed, clawed hands and feet tearing at the dirt.

Tunneling into the ground, Qing found breathing space in a mole's lair, even if he did have to argue briefly with the owner over his trespass. Given she'd almost lost her den to one of the soldiers' landing, Qing couldn't blame the poor thing for being upset.

Fortunately, Qing was intimidating enough to persuade the creature to be quiet. He'd pay her back when it was safe, he promised. For now, he had to get as far below ground as possible.

Before that old man, whoever he was, took him captive as well.

修炼

The shadow of the turtle moved off an hour or so after it'd arrived, taking Xinglu and Cui Wen with it. Their captors carried off the camping goods, making Qing glad he'd kept the crane-ship's controller when he'd escaped. Chasing an invisible turtle would be impossible without some sort of guide.

Holding the controller with his newly formed foreclaws, he swam through the sky, hoping to catch up unnoticed. He'd barely gotten started before he drew the attention of a local dragon, a young female who meant to remind him that territories existed and he wasn't supposed to be flying around when he hadn't even made it over the Dragon Gate.

"Ma'am, I promise you, I've no designs on your lake," he gasped as she flew circles around him. "I'm just passing through."

"There've been too many things passing through lately. Why should a jumped-up little fish who somehow managed to cultivate limbs use my sky for free?"

Qing pled, "I'm just chasing a turtle...."

"HAH! That's not a turtle. That's some stupid human's idea of a turtle."

"Fine! I'm chasing a statue of a turtle. Can you please, please, PLEASE let me through?" The sky around them crackled, startling the dragon.

"How the hell does a baby like you have weather control?" she demanded.

"I cultivated it."

She fell silent, flowing along beside him as he checked his controller and shifted his direction. "What is that thing?"

"That turtle statue swallowed my master's crane-ship. I'm following it."

"Why would a dragon have a crane-ship? Why would a dragon even need a crane-ship?"

Qing managed not to lose his temper. "My master isn't a dragon. I'm a disciple of the Book Hunters sect."

"Oh." Silence again, followed by, "Does you have anything by Moshiu? Or Ji Si?"

He rolled his eyes. "Of course. We sell dozens of copies wherever we go."

"I'll let you pass for three volumes of Villain's Reformation."

"You'll have to wait. I have to fetch my friends and get back to my Master first."

"If you make it five volumes, I'll help you." At his hesitation, she added, "I have a whole skeleton's worth of bones to pick with that stone turtle's master."

Qing was alone, didn't know if Xinglu and Cui Wen could help at all, and had no idea how to fight the sorcerer behind his friends' capture. He didn't like this dragon but he needed help. "All right, as long as you actually help, I can give you a whole set."

That excited the dragon. "I am Shi Huan, daughter of Shi Feng and Shi Ming of Bailu Lake. I swear by my pearl I'll do my best to aid you."

"Then I swear by my spirit stone that I will give you the books I've promised, as long as you do." There wasn't much left of his stone, of course, but it was enough to swear on at least.

She spun enthusiastically. "That old bastard is strong. That's why I've never tried to go after him. We'll need to be careful. And we have get him before he reaches his mountain."

"What's his name?"

"Zhu Kan."

That made Qing blink. "Zhu?" That was Cui Wen's real family name. So the turtle's master really was his friend's grandfather? If so, best not to mention it.

"Yes. He was Zhu Clan's leader before he sacrificed a whole family to improve his cultivation. The *jianghu* turned on him and trapped him in his fortress on Yaomei Peak. He uses that turtle and his statues to fetch whatever he wants."

No wonder Cui Wen was angry. Zhu Kan's greed for power had caused the attack on his family. "So there's no one inside the turtle at all?"

"Just statues under his control." Shi Huan sniffed. "Not something I'd like to go up against alone. With a too-smart dragon-carp who's coming into his power? An apprentice Book Hunter? Doable, if you have your tools and are willing to fight."

Of course, Qing was willing to fight. He hadn't run and hid because he was afraid, but to give himself a chance. "We'll try," he said, pushing himself to fly faster. They needed to hurry, and not just because he didn't know how his friends were doing. They couldn't afford to let Zhu Kan get them to his mountain.

Not when the old man might be a great deal stronger there.

修炼

They caught up with the stone turtle an hour later. The thing moved fast, requiring them to put on far more speed than either was accustomed to. They were both near exhaustion when they landed on the giant statue's shell.

Landing was an adventure in itself. Finding an invisible stone turtle was difficult. Finding and landing safely? Much harder. Without Qing's specialized sense they'd have missed or landed too hard. As it was, Shi Huan still nearly rolled straight off the thing's invisible surface.

When Qing turned human and caught her, she glared. "You have a human shape too? How?"

"I told you. I cultivated it. Everything I am, I cultivated."

She sniffed, sitting on his shoulders, clinging with all twelve claws. "Cultivated. What sort of cultivation do carp do in Khaitan?"

There was no way he'd explain to a dragon he hardly knew. He'd cultivated through that spirit stone and still had almost half the thing left over. That made him a particularly valuable treasure. Was that why Zhu Kan wanted him as well?

"Never mind. We need to find our way inside this thing." He climbed the shell, relying on his air-sense to tell where to step. Using his eyes was dangerous. By vision alone, he seemed to be walking on thin air, moving rapidly over a mountainous landscape.

Shi Huan muttered and grumbled the whole way. "How are you seeing where to go?"

"I'm using the air to sense where everything is."

"Air sense? Oh, you mean like water sensing?" At his agreement, Shi Huan sighed. "Lake dragons like me don't manage that terribly well. Good thing I can sit on your shoulder. What do you... see... then?"

"There's a building this way. I'm guessing the entrance is there. Zhu Kan's statues aren't anywhere around."

She considered that. "You should look for another way in. That building would be the main entrance. Don't you think it's heavily guarded?"

Surely any path inside would be heavily guarded? But she was right. Qing searched the turtle's surface for another way in. Nothing. "I agree it's dangerous, but I don't see any alternative."

"What about the mouth? You told me you think the turtle swallowed that crane-ship of yours."

Well, yes, but... Qing stopped himself. No reason why they couldn't try that path first. He hurried forward, trying to move as quietly and softly as he could, clambering along the stone turtle's neck and over its head. "We're going to have to fly in."

"That's too dangerous as fast as we're moving. The only reason the wind isn't taking us off right now is your weight. Do you have any climbing equipment?"

Every Book Hunter had their own Tool-Book, but Qing's wasn't as well stocked as Master Zhi's. "I don't."

"Right. I'll have to shapeshift to something larger."

Shi Huan forced her body to its largest form, an impressive ten feet worth of pale-blue scales. She crawled down, sticking her head inside the stone turtle's mouth. "I can see inside. It looks safe enough. Climb down me and jump in."

Qing did so carefully, maintaining his grip against an increasing breeze. Then he was inside the stone turtle's mouth, where the invisibility array no longer functioned. Inside was a long, dark, tunnel, with no light at its end.

He hesitated. Was he being too trusting again? What if Shi Huan were allied with Zhu Kan?

"Hey! Get your lovely scales moving, dragon-carp. I don't have all day."

Sighing, because second-guessing oneself was a dangerous exercise, Qing leaped into the darkness.

修炼

The end of Qing's leap slammed him into a rocky surface in a pitch-black room. A moment later Shi Huan crashed into him, and returned to her smaller form. A damned good thing, too. He couldn't have taken a half-ton of lake dragon.

Bruised. Aching. More than a little irritated, he tried not to growl. "Please be careful."

"Sorry. I slipped." She curled up on his shoulder, adding, "Do you have a light?"

Qing took a luminous night pearl from his *qiankun* pouch and raised it over his head. Immediately, Shi Huan squeaked and shifted to a larger form, ripping his outer robe with her talons as she slid off him, glaring upwards and growling.

He followed her gaze towards a huge black beak and intensely black eyes in a pale head. It neither moved nor reacted because it couldn't. "It's just Master Zhi's crane-ship." Qing shifted the light so he could inspect the tool for damage. "Good. He looks flightworthy still."

"Why the nine hells does your master use a crane puppet for a flying-ship?" Shi Huan sounded furious, glaring at the crane-ship as if she meant to rip it apart. "A plain boat isn't good enough for her?"

A plain boat flying through the sky would draw far more attention than a crane. Admittedly a crane this large risked notice, but most people just imagined the thing was nearer to the ground than it actually was. Qing didn't argue the point. "Let's see if we can find my friends."

"There's a doorway." Calmer, Shi Huan returned to Qing's shoulder. "Try not to make too much noise. We don't want to attract attention."

Resembling a naïve teenager with no sense in his head meant everyone and their sister felt he needed guidance. Qing tried not to grumble, glad of the company. This place was unnerving enough as it was.

They crept down the passage, Qing using his air-sense to tell what lay ahead. At first, the place appeared empty, a twisting corridor of seemingly endless side passages. No landmarks, nothing to give him any idea of where he should go. All there was, was grey stone, polished and lifeless.

"How are you finding your way?" Shi Huan demanded.

"I'm a Book Hunter. We're used to dealing with library stacks."

Shi Huan huffed irritably. "That doesn't make any sense."

"It does to me and I'm the one doing the walking. And what was that you said earlier about not making too much noise?"

She huffed, dropping the argument. "Can't you use that air-sense to explore instead?" she asked.

The passages were too twisted for that. Qing could get an idea of where he was, but couldn't spread his awareness far enough. "No." He paused. Sniffed the air. Raised a brow. "You're wrong that there's no books. I smell some ahead."

"You. Smell. Books."

"Haven't you ever been in a library before? Or around any books?"

"I'm a lake dragon. We don't go in for scholarship." She tapped one of her foreclaws together, reminding him that she only had three claws per foot. "The only thing that's important to me is my pearl."

There was an odd note of grievance to her tone. One that Qing didn't have time to question. "Never mind. Get ready for a fight."

"Why?"

"Unless I'm mistaken, there's a statue ahead, as well as those books. I think it's a guard." Lacking a better weapon, Qing drew on his *qi*, summoning lightning to his fingers.

Shi Huan scurried off his shoulder, crawling up the wall to the ceiling. She clung there, staying out of the line of sight, as they rounded the corner and came upon an open doorway. Qing air-sensed the stone guard beyond and smelled several dozen scrolls and books.

He hesitated, unsure if he should check the room or just move on. Book Hunter's instincts aside, Master Zhi's training said he shouldn't draw attention to himself. The books weren't going to run off on their own, after all. Except some books could and what if there was something important in there?

The decision was taken from him when Shi Huan - for reasons he didn't understand - slithered into the room. Hearing a crash, he sighed and stepped to the doorway, just in time to see Shi Huan take a large enough form to allow her to grab the stone guard and slam its head against the floor as hard as she could.

It shattered with the force of her blow and Qing made note not to let her get her claws on him in this shape. She could do his human body some damage if she felt like it. He'd survive, but it'd hurt. It might even break some bones.

"What are you doing?" Qing demanded as Shi Huan slithered through the storeroom, opening chests and pushing books to the floor. Most were weapons manuals; oddly mismatched and poorly maintained. He caught Shi Huan's mane and pulled her back. "Stop that and talk to me."

"Let me look." She pulled herself free of his grasp, unwilling to stop searching.

"You've just alerted Zhu Kan that we're here. Now we have to hurry."

She disagreed. "He can't maintain awareness of all his guards at once. He'll only notice this one's gone if he needs something from this storeroom."

"How do you know he won't need something?" Qing had thought of Shi Huan as the older and wiser big sister, someone to depend upon for common sense. Apparently, he was wrong. "Come on. We have to find my friends."

She grumbled, having satisfied herself that the thing she wanted wasn't there. "Fine. Let's go."

As they turned to leave, Qing noticed Cui Wen's work gloves on the floor, fallen from one of the boxes Shi Huan had rifled through. Likely they'd been shoved here for later inspection. He shoved them into his *qiankun* bag, planning on returning them as soon as they found Cui Wen.

"Stop wasting time. Let's go."

Trying not to lose his temper, Qing hurried back into the maze of corridors.

修炼

They found other storerooms and other guards. Rifled through other storerooms and destroyed other guards. Found other bits and pieces of Xinglu and Cui Wen's possessions, including Xinglu's qiankun pouch with Cui Wen's chair. All useful items Qing was glad to collect. None so pressingly required that it was worth the risk of drawing the enemy's attention.

"Why do you keep doing this?" Qing demanded.

"I need to find it." As ever, Shi Huan refused to explain what 'it' was. She just kept searching, growing more and more angry and desperate with each storeroom. "At least I'm getting rid of the guards."

"And what do you plan on doing when Zhu Kan notices and sends all of the guards he has left?" There'd been over a score of the things when Zhu Kan had taken Qing's friends captive. Shi Huan had only destroyed eight so far.

"We'll figure it out."

Oh, now it was 'we'? It was becoming blatantly obvious why Shi Huan had come with him on this mission. He should have told her to stay out of his business. Except she was older than he, a full dragon, and he was just a baby dragon-carp. Instinct and training had taught him to listen to his elders.

Something crashed ahead of them. A stone guard's head slammed into the wall some ten feet away and rolled off to the side. At the same time, a voice gasped, "Careful. There's someone just around the corner!"

Cui Wen? Qing sighed with relief. Of course, his friends wouldn't sit around waiting for rescue. He'd no clue how the pair had escaped Zhu Kan's clutches but he didn't care. "Xinglu? Cui Wen?" he called. "It's me!"

Xinglu rounded the corner, looking positively feral, his black sword glowing with an intense red heat. Cui Wen clung to his back tightly, looking more than a little worried. Seeing Qing, they both relaxed. "Oh. It is you. We should get out of here, then. You... ah... wouldn't happen to know the way out?"

Qing grinned. "Sorry to take so long coming to find you. I have all this help."

That made Shi Huan scoff. "I have my reasons."

"Which you haven't explained and which we don't have time to explore. How many guards are left, Xinglu?"

"I took down eight getting us out of here."

That left at least eight more. More than Qing wanted to deal with. He and Shi Huan were badly bruised already. Gods knew what'd happen when Zhu Kan really came after them.

"Let's get back to the crane-ship, then." When Shi Huan objected, Qing pointed out, "I came here for my friends. I don't have a good reason to stay and risk our lives. Our deal didn't include me playing your bodyguard."

"But...."

"No. You want to stay, that's fine. We're leaving."

"You're not going anywhere."

Zhu Kan's voice echoed through the halls of the stone turtle's insides as if the whole thing had spoken. As the walls set to shifting and opening out, Qing guessed it had. Apparently, he could speak through the turtle as well as his soldiers.

Xinglu swung his sword at the shifting wall, shattering it. "Which way, Qing? Point me at the exit!"

Qing examined his memorized map of the turtle's insides. Pointed. "The crane-ship's that way. Hurry!"

Striking again and again, blade dimming with every blow, Xinglu set to cutting a hole straight through the stone turtle's body and towards its 'stomach'. The shattered walls struggled to reshape, struggled to trap them, but Xinglu was faster, breaking through as they ran.

All Qing could do was hope they could break the crane-ship free once they reached it.

修炼

The crane-ship was tipped sideways, its legs broken, its wings badly scuffed by the tossing around it'd received. It could still fly, given Xinglu could manage a big enough hole. The boy's sword had dimmed measurably by the time they'd reached the thing and Xinglu himself looked exhausted.

"Sorry... I'm not sure I can... do this...." Xinglu sent blast after blast of sword *qi* slamming into the base of the chamber, while Qing, Shi Huan, and Cui Wen worked to keep the guards off them. Qing's lightning wasn't completely effective, but it, combined with Shi Huan's heavy blows and the small explosives from Cui Wen's weaponry, did enough to stave them off.

The trouble was, the hole Xinglu created wasn't nearly big enough for the crane-ship to fit. And fit it had to. With its legs ruined it wouldn't make it out of the turtle's mouth, even if Zhu Kan hadn't closed that exit already. Worse, their captor was using his power over the stone to reseal the hole Xinglu worked so hard to create.

Zhu Kan's voice shouted at them. "Don't think you can escape!"

Perhaps not, but Qing was in no mood to let the man win. He wasn't even there, for the Gods' sake. Qing didn't like the idea of losing. He most definitely didn't like the idea of losing to a giant stone turtle. He turned to Xinglu, pointing upwards. "I have an idea. Can you destroy the ceiling?"

"Not and break us free afterwards," Xinglu denied, leaning on his dimming sword exhaustedly.

"I have something." Cui Wen handed Qing a silver ball. "Be careful. It needs impact to work."

Qing shifted to his dragon-carp form, clinging to the explosive with one of his newly formed limbs. Then he swam upwards, aiming himself for the

" THE BOY'S SWORD DIMMED... "

spot right below where a real turtle's brain would be. The stone soldiers had all stopped working when their heads were destroyed. That meant the stone turtle, another of Zhu Kan's puppets, might break down too if the right place was damaged. Qing searched for the weakest point. Ah. Yes. There.

Pushing the silver ball into a crack, Qing swam downwards as far as he dared, then turned and loosed a bolt of lightning. It struck the ball, setting off the explosives within, shattering the stone surrounding it. Flung backward by the blast, Qing slammed into the floor of the chamber and lay still.

Deafened, Qing dimly heard shouting. Only when Shi Huan rushed to him, screaming, "It's going down!" did he understand the danger. He let her help him back to the crane-ship, even as Xinglu used the last of his strength to break open the floor and let the crane-ship fall through.

They dropped out of the hole and Qing hurriedly tossed the controller to Cui Wen. He didn't have the strength to do anything more. Getting them out of there would have to be on his friends.

The last thing Qing saw before he dropped unconscious was the stone turtle, hidden no more, crashing into a nearby mountain.

Chapter 5: Seeking Knowledge

Zhi Wenku glared. Tightened her lips. Tried not to growl. Somehow she succeeded, though the temptation to make her feelings known to everyone in the village, possibly everyone on the whole mountain, was painfully strong.

"Really," she asked, voice low and seemingly calm. "Can I not trust you to manage a simple errand without doing yourself and the surroundings permanent damage?"

Shen Wei's fan swung quietly in front of him, the words, 'dog house', forming on its surface. His gaze at Xinglu was no less meaningful than the one Zhi Wenku had turned on her own apprentice. "I notice you almost broke your seal in the process, wolfling," he told the boy.

Seal? No, that wasn't important right now. Zhi Wenku focused. "I'm waiting for an answer, child."

Qing gaped at her foolishly, looking as if his eyes would fall out of his head if he opened them any further. He even managed to resemble the carp he once was, as he tried to respond.

At last, he said, "I didn't look for the turtle. It looked for us. For him, I think." He pointed at Cui Wen, who had the grace to look embarrassed. "At least it sounded like that was what Zhu Kan wanted."

The name Zhu Kan meant nothing to Zhi Wenku but Shen Wei reacted sharply. "No one mentioned Zhu Kan. If he's involved why the devil didn't you say so? We need to know if he's escaped his fortress. And why would he want you, Young Master Cui?"

Cui Wen managed the weakest of smiles. "He's my grandfather and I'm my father's son." At Zhi Wenku's frown, he explained, "Zhu Kan used to be a respected sect leader. Except he executed the Song family, taking their *qi* in payment for a series of murders he claimed their leader instigated."

"Murders that were not, after all, the Song family's doing?" Zhi Wenku recognized the situation, if not the specifics. Gods knew it happened often enough, even in Khaitan.

"That's right. Song You, the only survivor, found proof the bandits were working for him. She attacked my family and killed them in retaliation. Well, most of them." Cui Wen gestured at himself. "I'm still not sure why she spared me."

Zhi Wenku seized on the only important point. "Why would you being your father's son matter to him?"

Before Cui Wen could answer, Shen Wei explained, "His father would have been Zhu Jianhong, Soul Protection Society's best machinist. Zhu Kan was always trying to get his son to come back and work for him instead. It seems he hoped to recruit his grandson, now he's grown."

"I see." This all involved local politics and wasn't Zhi Wenku's business unless someone here made it hers. Still, she was curious. "Would anyone care to explain why Cui Wen was aboard my crane-ship at all?"

"That's my fault," Cui Wen admitted. "I was afraid I'd be targeted by whoever was behind that sorcerer. I convinced Qing and Xinglu to bring me along. I didn't want to disrupt your efforts at finding a cure."

Yet another perfectly reasonable explanation that still left Zhi Wenku with a major problem. "I can't fault you for being concerned and you'd no way of knowing your grandfather would come after you. I'm glad you three escaped, not at all sure what to do with your new ally, and completely at a loss for what to do about the mess you made."

She gestured at her crane-ship, trying not to be depressed. Such vehicles were expensive and she'd just spent a great deal on a very necessary panacea. They'd have to repair the poor thing, the sooner the better. If they waited too long, what was left of the arrays powering its flight would fade away.

"Master Zhi? I can help with that if you're willing to let me." Cui Wen smiled at her, adding, "Since it was my presence that set everything off, it's the least I can do."

Having seen the boy's work, Zhi Wenku admitted he was capable enough. "Can you work quickly? We've almost solved the problem of that poison and the longer I stay here in Lian Village, the fewer sales I'm making."

"Told you she'd say that," Qing muttered.

Ignoring the sass, Zhi Wenku kept her gaze focused on Cui Wen. "Well?"

"If Qing and Xinglu help me, yes. I can do it in two weeks."

"One."

"One and a half. Don't rush something that's supposed to keep you in the air."

It wasn't as if they needed the crane-ship at the moment. Zhi Wenku could move on and stop in later to pick up the result. But if Cui Wen needed help and the boys were willing to assist, she supposed she couldn't disagree. She accepted the offer, pretending reluctance.

Turning her attention to the young lake dragon sitting on Qing's shoulder, Zhi Wenku continued, "As for you, young lady, based on what Qing told me, it seems the two of us will need to talk."

"Three," Shen Wei offered. "I admit to some concerns myself."

Eyes almost as wide and foolish as Qing's, Shi Huan agreed.

修炼

They went to the cave where the pixiu was resting, recovering from her ordeal with the western sorcerer's emetic. The villagers didn't go anywhere near the beast, despite being told the only things she ate were treasures. Even the sorcerer was gone, having been moved down to a local farm for a course of manual labor.

"Right. Now we're mostly alone, why don't you tell me just what it is you were looking for when you... helped... my apprentice."

Shen Wei's fan flickered the words, 'for varying definitions of help', as he waved it slowly in front of him. "And please don't give us any nonsense about wanting Moshiu's latest work."

That was another thing Zhi Wenku was going to have to talk to Qing about. Moshiu's novels were popular and frequently sold out. Getting a whole set would prove difficult. Zhi Wenku shook off the thought and refocused the conversation. "You were looking for something inside that turtle. The first question is, what?"

"First?"

"I also want to know why you want it and how dangerous whatever it is happens to be. Especially if it's a book."

The dragon sniffed. "I'm a lake dragon. We don't do books."

"Nonsense. Lake dragons are perfectly capable of educating themselves. Perfectly capable of protecting their books from water, for that matter. Why else bargain for them from my apprentice?"

Shi Huan flinched. Apparently, she hadn't thought of that. "I didn't mean I don't read. Just that I don't go in for scholarship."

That was because she was still terribly young. Too young to be on her own. She might be older than Qing by a good century, but she was still a baby by dragon standards. "Where are your parents?"

"Don't know." The young dragon sniffed. "I'm fine on my own. Dragons don't have to have adults to survive."

Shi Huan was likely right. Trueborn dragons were tough creatures, with innate knowledge most beings lacked. Still, "An adult isn't there just to keep you alive, child. They're there to teach you how to meet the world. So far you haven't done the best of jobs."

That made Shi Huan bristle. "What do you mean?"

Sounding amused, Shen Wei asked, "May I?" At Zhi Wenku's agreement, he waved his fan, changing the characters to 'First mistake'. "You attacked a stranger for flying above your territory. If Qing had been swimming in your lake you'd have been in your rights. He wasn't and he was clearly just flying through."

She sank. "I don't like strangers near my territory."

The fan showed the words, 'Second Mistake'. "When Qing refused to fight, you forced him to bribe you to let him go, even though you had no justification for interfering with him.'

"I like Moshiu's books."

Another wave. Another word change: 'Third Mistake'. "You chose to join him in the attempt to save his friends, making him think you were older and wiser than he and could be relied upon for guidance. Only to prove you were neither when you entered the stone turtle and set to searching it for your own purposes instead."

A sigh. "I am older than he is."

"Age and maturity aren't the same thing, young lady," Zhi Wenku told her firmly. "There's some Immortals who can't be trusted to dress when they go out."

Now the dragon pouted. "I just...."

"You just wanted something you thought might be aboard that stone turtle. What?"

Mumbling, Shi Huan stared at the ground. At Zhi Wenku's impatient 'hmmm?' she said a little louder, "He stole my pearl. Zhu Kan did."

Ah. Now everything made sense. Trueborn dragons hatched clutching the spirit pearl that assisted in their cultivation. It functioned as a Golden Core, allowing them to maintain a vast reservoir of *qi* even as a child. Only when they were adults, and able to contain the raw power within their bodies, did they absorb the thing into their forehead.

Shen Wei considered that carefully. Then, "What happened to your parents, child?"

Curling in on herself, looking about as small as she could, Shi Huan said, "I don't know. Gone. They went hunting and never came back. I thought it was fun, and it was for a while, but then that man stole my pearl and I couldn't get to him or chase his stone turtle when it's invisible. So...."

"So when you found someone else who was also chasing the stone turtle and had a way to track it, you latched onto him." Zhi Wenku understood the young dragon's reasoning now. "You should have told him the truth."

"He's just a baby! And a dragon-carp at that! He doesn't even have a pearl!"

Ah, yes. Zhi Wenku had forgotten that trueborn dragons looked down on dragon-carps like Qing, though they pretended otherwise. Without any adult to teach her better manners, it was no wonder Shi Huan had let her prejudices affect her judgment.

"Dragon-carp put their lives and souls on the line to pass the Dragon Gate, child. Qing has been diligently cultivating ever since he first formed a foundation. Did your parents teach you to devalue hard work and effort?"

A faint flush formed beneath Shi Huan's scales. "I... no... they didn't. I'm sorry. I'll apologize to him."

"A good idea. And then, since you're so interested in what's inside that stone turtle, why don't you come along with us once my crane is fixed." At Shi Huan and Shen Wei's curious expressions, Zhi Wenku continued, "Qing told me the thing was full of old manuals. Most probably aren't of interest to my sect but all could be valuable to someone. I intend to find out."

Because the one thing she'd never do was abandon books to the elements.

修炼

It was one and a half weeks exactly before Zhi Wenku's crane-ship was repaired and ready for flight. Ordinarily she'd put the ship away and travel by foot, but she wanted to get to the crash-site quickly before the books aboard the turtle were irreparably damaged.

Besides, she and Qing weren't alone this time. Shen Wei had asked to come along, saying, "We knew Zhu Kan was up to something, despite being bound to his mountain. This is the first time we've gotten a clue to how. I want a look at what's left of that stone turtle."

If Shen Wei came, so did Xinglu. So, too, did Cui Wen and Shi Huan, the one because he still needed protection, the other in the unlikely hope of finding her pearl in the stone turtle's remains. The only reason she hadn't stayed and searched the wreckage earlier was the debt she owed Qing. She'd made sure he got to safety before doing anything else.

That much proved she'd had a decent upbringing, even if she'd been alone the last fifteen years. Zhi Wenku had no intention of inviting her to come along permanently, but she was less out of sorts with the young dragon than she might have been.

The stone turtle had crashed in a remote mountainous area, not terribly far from Khaitan's border. According to Shen Wei, Zhu Kan's mountain prison was just a day's flight off to the southwest. "We have guards on it, of course, but we didn't know he had such a tool or any sort of invisibility spell."

That invisibility spell was well and truly ruined, along with the turtle. It was broken in half, its head buried in the side of the mountain, its back-end broken off and slid upside-down into the valley. Qing called back from his post atop the crane's head, "You see, master? I told you I didn't think that map you made me draw would be much use."

"Sassy carp-child," she told him. "It can still help. At least it can help with the back half. The front's pretty well destroyed."

They all gazed at the mess in agreement. The turtle had hit the ground head first and that had taken the full brunt of the blow. The front flippers were broken off, the carapace crushed and the head had crumbled into small pieces. There were strange things inside the remains, similar to the devices Cui Wen made.

The boy pointed to them. "I think that's why he wanted me. He's a puppet master, but he couldn't make them move without the right internal structure."

Spiritual puppetry was not a thing Zhi Wenku understood, but one thing she did know. Something like this needed a power source. "How did he keep it moving? You said his prison's close, but the turtle was a good half-day north of here when it chased down my crane-ship. Is there any chance he could have been aboard?"

Shen Wei frowned. "I don't think so. The prison array surrounding his mountain is quite strong. It won't let any living thing in or out."

The key word was 'living'. Zhi Wenku couldn't guess how Zhu Kan controlled his stone turtle but having no living crew it must have passed the prison array easily. "I wonder how he proposed to get Xinglu and Cui Wen to him. Your array would have stopped him."

"A good question and one I've no answer to. I'll have to send word to my superiors, Zhu Kan being out of my area of expertise. Before that, though, shall we take a look inside the turtle's hind-end?"

Shi Huan made a little questioning noise and when Zhi Wenku and Shen Wei looked at her, asked, "Could I search the front? Just in case my pearl's in there?"

"Will your pearl be all right? There's not much left of the head now."

A little fang-toothed smile. "It's part of me. I'd know if it was destroyed."

Zhi Wenku considered the request. "We'll check that together. No one wanders off alone. Not when we've no idea if Zhu Kan can still do anything."

Seeing no disagreement, she set off up the slope to the crumbled remains of the turtle's front half.

修炼

Cui Wen managed the uphill climb by altering the shape of his chair, making it a framework that supported his body and let him 'walk' after a fashion. He still needed Xinglu and Qing to steady him on the soft uneven ground, but the chair proved his claim to be very much his father's son. Zhi Wenku knew little about such things but she recognized a triumph of mechanistic craftsmanship when she saw it.

The mechanisms inside the turtle's head drew Cui Wen like a moth to a flame. Like any obsessed talent, he insisted on examining each gear, lever and chain. "This looks like my father's work," he said, distressed. "But that can't be. Can it?"

"Do you mean it looks like his designs? Or something he built by his own hands?"

"It's his design, at least. I'm not sure if it's his handiwork." Cui Wen picked up one of the pieces and searched around the coppery-bronze metal. Then he breathed a sigh of relief. "Any decent machinist can follow another's design. But we all mark our pieces, so we know whose work it is. See?"

Shen Wei tilted his head, looking at the tiny scratches at the edge of the gear, a simple elegant flower Zhi Wenku couldn't identify. Shen Wei recognized it, though, saying, "But that is your father's mark."

"It's his mark but not his hand." Cui Wen pulled off his work glove to show the same mark on the corner of the metal band. "See, father always crossed this line over this and put extra pressure on this petal."

Zhi Wenku understood. "It's like our copyists. The work is supposed to be identical but you can always tell whose it is by the way they lay their strokes."

"Right. My grandfather might have used father's designs but father didn't help him build this thing." The relief in the boy's voice was palpable. "When Song You killed my family, she burned most of our house in the process. There's no way to count the dead. I... feared my father might be alive and helping grandfather."

What a terrible thing, to have to hope a deceased parent was dead, rather than helping an evil man's evil deeds. Lacking words, Zhi Wenku set her hand on the boy's shoulder, squeezing gently.

After a moment Cui Wen sighed and smiled. "We'd best keep looking for clues. Besides, Shi Huan must be anxious to find her pearl."

The young dragon was pacing back and forth across Qing's shoulders by now. At some point someone was going to have to teach her manners. She was doing a good job controlling the urge to either run ahead or snap at them to hurry, but her impatience was obvious.

They continued up the slope amid the debris until they reached the largest chunk of rock, a solid piece of granite, with a huge eye carved out of it. That eye moved as they approached, shifting sideways just enough to make it clear it saw them. "It's still alive?" Qing gasped. "How can it still be alive?"

"Not alive," Xinglu corrected, sniffing the air as if he could smell the ambient *qi*. "I would have sensed it was alive when it started chasing us. It's just a puppet."

"Then why is it moving? Aren't its strings cut?" Qing poked at the eye, causing it to twitch and turn towards him in what would be a glare if it could have managed one.

Sighing, Zhi Wenku caught his hand. "Don't poke at things, Qing. Remember what happened with General Shi."

"Oh. Yes. Sorry."

Turning her attention to Shen Wei, Zhi Wenku asked, "Is it possible for Zhu Kan to still be controlling this thing? Can he hear us?"

"I'm an alchemist, not a puppet master." Shen Wei examined the eye carefully. "I think he could see through it. Or it could still have some energy left from whatever he used to power it. I really don't know how such things work."

"Let's keep searching, then. And, everyone, if you find a part that still moves, treat it respectfully. We don't know how the turtle was being controlled." Zhi Wenku set to examining the pieces of broken rock, having Qing pick up the larger chunks so she could check underneath.

It took almost an hour but they slowly pieced together the shape of the turtle's head. It took Qing and Shi Huan and Xinglu together to move some of those chunks but they finally had some idea of where the 'brain' of the thing would have been.

"There's a hollow here," Qing noted, once they'd finished. "About this big. I don't think it would have been your pearl, Shi Huan." He held his fingers two inches apart. "It's too small for that, right?"

Shi Huan held out a clawed hand, bending her fingers slightly as if she were holding a large sphere. "My pearl's this big, so no. It wouldn't have fit." She sighed. "I don't know if I'm relieved or sorry."

"Small blame to you, either way," Zhi Wenku told her. "If it was inside that hole it'd be destroyed by now. That or fallen out."

Shi Huan agreed. "I don't like this."

None of them liked this and they all knew it. Zhi Wenku was about to suggest turning back to the less badly damaged part of the stone turtle when Cui Wen asked, "What's this thing?" He held up a small gold object about the size of a pheasant's egg. "It's soft. I pressed on it just now and my weight didn't do it any damage."

Not an egg. Not stone, either, as far as Zhi Wenku could tell. "Shen Wei? Do you recognize this thing?"

The alchemist carefully took the sphere from Cui Wen. His lips tightened as he pressed on its surface. "It feels like a core. A spiritual core." Taking a deep breath he added, "And it should not be possible."

He was right. A spiritual core was formed of condensed *qi*, solidified by cultivationists in the course of their meditations. They didn't survive outside the owner's body for long. "Are you sure?"

"You're a cultivationist, too. Touch it."

Zhi Wenku did so and agreed; it felt horribly wrong. She'd long since cultivated her own spiritual core and knew the solid, dense, feel of the material within her. She'd also dealt in spiritual stones. None had that soft, almost slimy, feel to them. "What is it, then?"

"That I can't answer. Not without more to go on. But it wouldn't surprise me if this gave the stone turtle its motive force." Shen Wei put the stone in a small box and stored it in his sleeve. "I doubt we'll find anything more up here. We should probably explore the other half now. I know you must be anxious for those books Qing saw."

Though Shen Wei was teasing her, he was also quite right. "Indeed. The sooner we get to them, the sooner we can go about our business."

Seeing no argument, she turned and headed back down the slope towards the rest of the stone turtle.

修炼

"I never asked the last time we were in here, but why aren't there any lights?"

Zhi Wenku considered Shi Huan's question, holding up a luminous night pearl to examine the walls of the corridor. Smooth. A great deal smoother than possible by standard building techniques. The material was the same everywhere, granite or something similar, polished to a matte finish, barely reflecting the dim light.

"I think those statues you fought don't need it to see."

Cui Wen scoffed. "Everything that sees needs light."

"Then they sense without seeing. Or see by a light we can't. Does it actually matter?"

No one had an answer to that, so they kept searching the passages. "Did you meet anyone other than statues in here?" Shen Wei asked his apprentice.

"No. Zhu Kan talked to us, the same way he did when he captured us, but he never said anything useful. Just that he "looked forward to finally seeing his grandson again". That and he expected Qing to show up any time.

Now that was interesting. "If he expected Qing, why wasn't he prepared for him?"

"I think that's because I made him go in through the mouth." Shi Huan gestured towards the front half of the stone turtle. "We didn't trust the building on the turtle's back."

Wait. There was a building? The turtle had gone belly up when it'd crashed, so all they'd seen so far had looked like a normal, if gigantic, turtle. "What building?"

"It was right at the top of the shell, master. We never actually went inside." Qing flushed, clearly realizing he'd failed to give Zhi Wenku every last detail of their escape. "And it was invisible, like the rest of the turtle, so all I could sense was its shape. I couldn't feel anything living inside so I didn't pay it much mind."

Likely a good thing. Based on the description it probably was a trap of some sort. Anyone finding the turtle would search for the highest spot. Finding, or feeling, a building would have seemed like a miracle. "You should have mentioned it earlier."

"Ah. Yes. Apprentice is wrong." Qing flushed with embarrassment.

"Where did they hold you, Xinglu?" Shen Wei's fan showed the words, 'Another thing to mention earlier'.

Now it was Xinglu who looked embarrassed. "Towards the center, below that building Qing mentioned. It's just an empty room, with a set of stairs leading into the dungeon."

Really, these boys needed remedial lessons on how to properly report on adventures. All of this might have been important and would have been best told long before they reached this point. Zhi Wenku and Shen Wei shouldn't have to pry information out of their disciples.

This not being the time to discuss the matter, Zhi Wenku decided, "I'll want to see if there's anything important in that building but let's concentrate on searching the storerooms."

They continued through the halls, following Qing's guidance. The child had done well on that count, memorizing every last detail of what he'd seen the last time he'd been here. It meant they didn't have to wander aimlessly, once they worked out where in Qing's mental map they were.

Having the upper half of the stone turtle buried in the mountainside complicated matters. The fact that Qing hadn't explored the entire thing didn't help either. Still, they found several storerooms and packed away everything they found in Zhi Wenku's Warehouse for later examination.

"If there's anything I envy about you Book Hunters, it's your packs," Shen Wei noted as they carried the last of their latest find through the Warehouse entrance. "Living things don't usually survive in *qiankun* items. This would be terribly useful if you're being hunted and need to hide."

Given that was one reason Warehouses were built that way, Zhi Wenku smiled. "We don't steal, but there's those who'd steal from us. We..."

A sudden crash outside, followed by Qing and Xinglu both calling out, "MASTER!" made her sigh and roll her eyes. She was just enjoying a quiet conversation. Why did every quiet conversation she had time for end with a crash?

Cui Wen, who'd paused to leaf through a book of machinist designs, turned a wide-eyed gaze on Zhi Wenku. "Ma'am? Should I...."

"Stay in here."

"But...."

"Both you and Shi Huan stay in here. If there's trouble I want you as backup. Wait until you're needed."

Once she was sure the pair would obey, Zhi Wenku and Shen Wei hurried out of the Warehouse, stepping back into the storeroom to find it a great deal fuller than it'd been before. "I suppose I should have expected this."

"We all should have."

After all, at least some of Zhu Kan's statues had to have survived. Zhi Wenku just wished there weren't quite so many of them. Fighting five or six or even eight might have been doable.

A full dozen? Far too many for the four of them to handle.

修炼

The statues didn't talk. Didn't explain their purpose. They also refused to take 'no' for an answer. Zhi Wenku and her companions would go where they were told without argument or someone would be hurt. Unable to fight, they were chivied through the upside-down halls and into the remains of that temple Xinglu had mentioned.

The building atop the back of the turtle had been driven deep into the mountainside. Its upper half had broken off and its interior was full of shattered pieces of rock.

A pair of wooden legs stuck out of the dirt, bare to the world as they flailed helplessly. A silk robe fell around the legs, the brightly colored brocade bearing symbols Zhi Wenku knew would get a human wearer executed for treason. "Are the Zhu family related to the emperor?"

"Even if they were, they aren't close enough to permit them to wear a five-toed dragon," Shen Wei remarked while the legs waved around even more furiously. One of the stone statues pushed them towards the legs, making it clear what was expected.

Zhi Wenku glanced toward Shen Wei, and saw him sigh resignedly.

Really, they weren't in a good position to fight. Cooperation was still necessary and would be for a bit longer. "All right," she snapped when one of the stone soldiers pushed her a bit harder than before. "We understand."

They set to digging the puppet out of the debris. Xinglu found a detached arm off to one side and Qing dug out the head. An old man's face glared at them in the dim light, trying to look fierce and failing because it was so covered in dirt and broken bits of wood that it looked more like the head of a well-used training dummy.

Qing set the head down to the side. "Oh, do stop cursing when you don't have a voice to curse with. You're just wasting your time."

A tiny squeak of rage managed to make itself heard. That was all the head could do, however, though not for the lack of trying. Zhi Wenku ignored it, continuing the effort at getting the main body free of the dirt.

At last, the thing popped out, pulled free so fast Zhi Wenku and Shen Wei tumbled to the ground before they could catch themselves. Maintaining her poise, Zhi Wenku brushed herself off and fetched the head. "This would be what you wanted," she asked, knowing the answer already.

The head made another of those noises and she turned towards the statue, holding the head tightly between her hands. As she walked she set her foot down on a piece of loose gravel and pretended to slip. Her fingers slid up through the neck, grasping at the inner workings.

There was a sudden shriek as she caught hold of something small, round, and unpleasantly squishy. Then the head fell silent, closely followed by the statues falling over around them. Zhi Wenku smiled, holding up the sphere she'd pulled from the wooden head. "Thought so," she said. "Gentlemen, I do believe we've found this thing's motive force."

Just as the others were about to react, the room they stood in shook. Shuddered. Jolted around sharply. There was a blinding flash of light, quickly followed by a deafening crash. Zhi Wenku clutched the dirt beneath her, trying to stand and unable to do so, as her stomach seemed to drop several hundred feet down.

Moments later the entire room turned right side up again, dropping them to the floor. Late afternoon sunlight streamed through the windows and a howling wind roared in their ears as they struggled to hang on. Flung sideways by the motion, they slammed into the walls of the room, Xinglu tumbling out an open doorway before anyone could do anything to help him. Half-stunned, Shen Wei almost fell after him, but Zhi Wenku caught him in time.

Before she could give the order, Qing shapeshifted, flinging himself out the window just as the room spun into a cloud. All Zhi Wenku could do was hope her apprentice reached the boy before he hit anything below. They were too high up for a human child to withstand such a fall.

Helpless, too disoriented to escape, Zhi Wenku clung to the wall and her Warehouse, stomach reeling. She could hardly see her hands in front of her face, much less her companion in misery. She waited, guessing where they were headed, hoping the ride would be over soon.

Hoping, too, Zhu Kan remembered that his prison didn't allow anything living to cross the barrier surrounding it. The last thing she wanted was to be smashed flat because her captor was too stupid to recall important details.

Chapter 6: Searching for Lost Masters

Qing spotted Xinglu spiraling down towards the ground and raced after him, catching the other boy's hand in his mouth, straining desperately to slow Xinglu's fall. His friend was only semi-conscious, half-stunned by the force of the blow that'd sent him flying earlier. It didn't help that Xinglu was all muscle and solid bone.

Slowing Xinglu's fall strained everything Qing had but he managed it, dropping into the forest below. They landed hard, crashing through tree branches, into the snow and several irritated rabbits. Fortunately for all concerned, they barely nudged the poor animals, though you couldn't have told that for the way they cursed him and Xinglu.

It took Xinglu a moment to recover enough to talk. "Thanks," he gasped. "I could have broken something."

Given how far they'd fallen, Xinglu would have done worse than break something. Humans were a great deal more fragile than spirit beasts after all. Qing didn't argue the point. "Are you hurt at all?"

"Only my pride and Master says I could do with a few bruises there. You?"

Qing checked himself. "Same and same."

That made Xinglu laugh. "Qing, you're the least arrogant spirit beast I've ever met."

That almost hurt Qing's feelings. He was a dragon-carp, with expectations of becoming a dragon by sheer force of will. Surely that was pure hubris in itself when a born fish sought to claim the skies?

When he said so, Xinglu turned serious. "I'm sorry, Qing. I didn't mean it that way. But you've earned the right to your pride. I've seen too many think blood or fortune made them right." He patted Qing's shoulder. "Now, let's figure out where we are and where the others are."

The first was easy enough. Qing flew into the air again, scanning the mountains below him and comparing them to the map he'd memorized of the area. "We're ten miles south of where the stone turtle crashed," he said when he'd returned to the ground. "And it's getting towards late afternoon. Should we find a place to camp?"

Xinglu considered the question, drawing his sword to fly on. "The sooner we catch up, the better. I don't know how it is with your Master, but mine has a talent for falling into the worst possible situations."

To tell the truth, Qing was the one usually guilty of that charge and he admitted it. "Any thoughts on which way to go?"

"Seems obvious Zhu Kan wanted to bring us to him. Gods know how he proposed getting us past the prison array or all the guards, but we were headed straight towards Yaomei Peak. That's our best choice for the moment."

Having no better idea, Qing agreed.

修炼

It was growing dark by the time Yaomei Peak came into sight, its crags surrounded by several other mountains, the other sisters in the small family of peaks.

A sudden draft flung Qing backward, knocking him so far that he almost lost control of his body and slammed into another mountainside. If Xinglu hadn't caught him by a proto-claw and tugged him upright he probably would have done exactly that.

"What was that?"

"I'm not sure." They stared around. "Definitely not natural," Xinglu said grimly. "Wind doesn't rise straight up like this." He pointed at the trees below them. "See their branches?"

Qing spotted Xinglu's meaning immediately, despite the dim light. There was a band where the trees were impossibly upright, their branches raised high and tight against their trunks as if the wind were blowing straight up from the ground.

"What is it?" he asked.

"A swordfall array by the feel of it. Likely intended to keep people from

"ARE YOU HURT AT ALL?"

getting to Zhu Kan's mountain." Xinglu headed for the ground. "We're not getting past that."

Qing had never come across such a thing before, but it wasn't hard to guess how it worked. Afoot or in flight, no one could break past a wind that blew so fast. They'd have to go around and hope their masters had been taken somewhere outside the circle.

"Isn't this too much? I thought they had an array on Yaomei Peak to keep living creatures from leaving or getting in," Qing complained as they flew.

Before Xinglu could answer, a woman's voice spoke from inside the band of wind. "We do." The words were quickly followed by a dozen or so darts, flying out at Qing and Xinglu so fast they barely had time to dodge. "Not that that stops fools like you trying to get past."

An older woman in black faded into view, floating through the wind with every hair and robe in perfect and pristine condition as if the gale had no business touching her. "Surrender, children, and I may not hurt you."

Qing spun round, diving into the trees. More darts followed him but his scales were too hard. The things bounced off and disappeared. At the same time, Xinglu soared high and higher, disappearing from view in the shadowed sky.

"Come back here!"

That shout came from below, from a woman in white robes, her fingers playing ruthlessly across a *qin*, sending sound *qi* after Xinglu.

Sound *qi* was something Qing understood, though. He focused his energies, sending a roll of thunder crashing across the mountainside, a ball of lightning rolling slowly down the hill towards the woman. At the same time, he shifted to his smallest size and slipped into the trees.

Yet again he hid instead of fighting. Infuriating, given his yearning to be more than a quivering child hiding beneath a rock. But Master Zhi had taught him to choose his battles and this wasn't one he could fight. Besides, he'd be in the wrong if he harmed either of these women. They were obviously Zhu Kan's prison guards. No need to start a feud between Qing's sect and theirs.

The wind cultivator rose into the sky, chasing after Xinglu, only to be thrown backward by a blast of raging fire. "DEMON!" she shouted. "YOU DARE?"

Qing remembered what Master Shen Wei had said about Xinglu breaking his seal and suddenly understood why the other boy was so strong despite his youth. Xinglu was part spirit beast, likely descended from one of the more monstrous of his kind. Cultivators outside Khaitan tended to equate them with demons, especially the more dangerous sort.

"Baby dragon," the woman in white crooned. "Come out, come out. You can't hide forever." Her music changed, becoming a hypnotizing song that floated around Qing, drawing at his mind, almost forcing him to obey.

As his body slipped down the trunk to the ground below, he realized 'almost' was wrong. Without even realizing it he'd been caught. A moment later a gentle hand scooped him out of the snow, slid him into a hollowed gourd, and capped it before he could recover enough to break free.

修炼

Qing curled grumpily in darkness, considering his options, unable to hear or see much of what was going on outside the gourd he'd been trapped in. He'd attempted breaking free by growing, but the gourd's walls were covered in protective seals, blocking his *qi* and muting his power.

He didn't think he was in danger. The cultivator in white could have injured him badly if she'd meant him harm. The trouble was, he didn't think either woman would listen to his pleas to be released, or believe his story if he told it.

A muffled noise drew his attention. A banging sound against the side of his gourd. He scrambled towards it, listening closely, and realized he could hear a familiar voice shouting, as if from a great distance. "LET ME OUT OF HERE YOU...."

What followed were the kind of words Qing wasn't allowed to use with anyone. But Xinglu had spent his childhood on the streets. No doubt he was just as frustrated as Qing. Just as trapped, as well.

There was another sound, this one louder than Xinglu's shouts and bangs. It was accompanied by the gourd spinning around the way that damned temple of Zhu Kan's had. Lucky thing Qing had a strong stomach or he might have been sick all over the place.

As it was he was disoriented and slammed against the sides of his prison, then tumbled upside down against the cap. When things stopped moving he lay still and tried to work out just what'd happened. Then, realizing the cap had loosened, he pushed and pushed and pushed with all his barbels and his claws, using his lower limbs to hold his body in place while he shoved.

The cap came free faster than Qing expected. He tumbled out onto wooden flooring, blinking confusedly before scanning his surroundings. A room, plain and austere, its contents flung around wildly by his captors and a half-dozen women in long pale robes, gloves, and masks. When one of their two captors ripped an intruder's robe, however, it revealed an arm formed of carved wood and paper-mâché.

"Puppets?" Qing muttered to himself, puzzling over the thing's appearance. "Where'd they come from?"

Seeing a puppet about to nail the cultivator in black to the floor with a lance, Qing shifted to his human form and slammed into the being, grabbing the lance from the puppet's hands. He rolled backward to give himself some distance. Rose to his feet. Slammed his borrowed weapon straight through the thing's belly, pinning it to the wall. If it were alive he'd have been more careful. He was less concerned with thing of wood, paper, and cloth.

It wriggled helplessly and he remembered how Master Zhi had dealt with the head of the puppet in the temple. He pulled the mask from the puppet's wooden skull, then caught hold of a too-soft golden blob. As the thing screeched and went still, another puppet turned to aim at him, only to be cut in half by wind *qi* summoned by the black-clad cultivator. Qing didn't hesitate to pull this one's mask off and remove its power source as well.

He checked his surroundings quickly. Noticing the gourd Xinglu was trapped in what was at his feet, he picked it up and undid the cap before either cultivator could stop him. "Sorry," he said, seeing their dark expressions, "But he is my friend after all."

As a large and angry fire-dog landed on the ground between them, he hoped he hadn't made a mistake.

修炼

It took several minutes to calm Xinglu enough to redraw his seal. He was a strong cultivator but not strong enough to remain in human form without assistance. Given the fire hazard he represented, Qing quite understood why Master Shen had been irritated with him earlier.

He understood, too, why their two captors were on edge. Their hut was wood and they were in the middle of a forest. If Xinglu truly lost his temper he could set the whole mountain alight. Fortunately, despite provocation, the half-spirit beast did his best to wait quietly for Qing to paint the seal.

Once that was done, Qing made his friend sit and be quiet. "Let me handle the explanations," he ordered. "You're too angry and we don't have time to fight."

He turned to the cultivators, desperately grateful that the white-clad one had restrained her partner. "Cultivators," he said, bowing politely, "This one is Qing, apprentice to Master Zhi Wenku of the Zang Shanghu."

"Book Hunters," the woman in white said calmly. "We've heard of you."

"Nonsense," the woman in black argued. "Why would a Book Hunter take a dragon-carp as an apprentice? And how the hell do you have a human form already at your age?"

Qing forced back a sigh. This wasn't the time to argue about his age or his skills or his apprenticeship. "The Zang Shanghu does not discriminate over age or species. Nor is it my place to argue with my master's decision to take me as an apprentice."

"Huo San, he's right. Don't be rude."

"He's just a baby, Li Tang. He should be chasing crumbs in a fishbowl, not playing with a devil dog like that one." The woman in black, Huo San, gestured at Xinglu, who curled a lip at her and allowed a bit of smoke to trail from one nostril.

Feeling it was unfair that he, of all people, had to play adult when there were two full-grown cultivators in the room, Qing told his friend, "Stop that. I just fixed your seal and I'm not nearly strong enough to have it hold if you push at it."

To Xinglu's credit, he apologized. "It's just so damned irritating to get that load of one-legged ox crap tossed at me all the time. Master Shen is willing to trust me. She's no right to insult him or me."

The cultivator named Huo San peered at Xinglu. "You claim to be Shen Wei's disciple? Where's your Society tablet?" When he grasped for his belt and went white, she sneered. "A pretty lie, then. I expected as much."

"After all the tossing around you gave me, how do you expect me to still have my tablet!? Besides, I'm sure you've heard about me."

Li Tang set a hand on her partner's arm. "Huo San, Master Alchemist Shen did take a half-spirit beast disciple just a year ago. And his robes have Soul Protection Society arrays woven in."

For a moment Qing feared the woman would shake Li Tang off and go on the attack. Then, sniffing, she snapped, "It must be trying, having to follow that man around. Keeping him supplied with grilled meats alone is troublesome enough."

Now it was Xinglu's turn to sneer. "Can you be any more obvious?" he demanded. "Everyone in the Society knows Master Shen's love is for sweet rice dumplings."

"Everyone in the society," Huo San agreed. "He doesn't indulge in front of outsiders. All right. You're who you claim. What I don't understand is why you and this little carp are wandering on your own. Particularly this close to Zhu Kan's prison."

Qing asked, "Unless I miss my guess, you're protecting the wind array surrounding Yaomei Peak." Seeing agreement, he continued, "Master Shen mentioned wondering how Zhu Kan is still causing problems for the martial world when he's trapped inside several layers of protection. I think I know."

Huo San eyed him. "You Book Hunters are always solving interesting puzzles," she admitted. "So what's your explanation for this one?"

Quickly, Qing told the pair about the stone turtle that'd chased them on their return from Khaitan, how it'd crashed and how they'd gone to investigate the site. "Zhu Kan must be controlling the stone turtle and those soldiers of his through his cultivation. It must be too big and dense for your wind to stop. And since it and the soldiers are puppets, the array blocking living creatures can't stop it either."

Looking enlightened, Li Tang said, "Remember that shadow I saw last month? The one we decided was a cloud or a roc? What if it was the turtle instead?"

"It... might have been. But you said it's destroyed, so why are you wandering around outside the wind array?"

"Because we got caught by Zhu Kan's puppets and carried off. I was thrown free, Qing here came to help me and our masters are somewhere out there, possibly in danger." Xinglu's eyes narrowed as he glared at Huo San. "And. You. Are. Wasting. Our. Time."

Hushing his companion, Qing added, "The two of us escaped but our masters didn't. We have to find them."

Doubt still flickered in Huo San's eyes and she pointed at the puppets that'd just attacked. "And these things? They're dressed in Bingyuan Sect robes."

Unsure about what Bingyuan Sect was, Qing showed her the blobs he'd taken from the puppets. "There was something like this in the turtle's head and another in Zhu Kan's puppet. If I had to guess, it's how he's manipulating his tools."

Li Tang took the blob, making a disgusted face as she manipulated it between her fingers. "It feels like a spiritual core. But it's too soft."

"I don't know how something like this could be created, but I think these things empower the puppets to move. They have to be designed to do so, of course." Qing pulled a puppet's sleeve back, revealing the metal bones and wires supporting and controlling the thing's limbs.

"You're telling me a thing like that could fight like a true cultivator?" Disbelief soared in Huo San's voice.

Before Xinglu could snap, Li Tang gently said, "Isn't it obvious it did?" As her partner went quiet, biting her lip embarrassedly, the white-clad cultivator said, "There've been kidnapping cases that looked like Zhu Kan's work for the last year. He couldn't bring his captives into his prison, not with the inner array blocking him, but now I wonder; could he take them to Bingyuan Sect?"

"Master Li, your pardon, but what sect is that?" Qing and his master mostly focused on finding certain lost books and selling others. They seldom had much to do with the martial world.

"They're a secluded group, all female," Xinglu told him before either Huo San or Li Tang could answer. "Very private. Very exclusive. They use the cold to help chill their lusts and calm their souls... at least that's what they claim."

"Is your name Master Li?" Qing couldn't help asking, a question that got his hair thoroughly ruffled. Returning his attention to the cultivationists, he added, "Then their sect is somewhere near?"

"They have a temple on Erguniang Peak. It was there before Zhu Kan took over Yaomei, though. So we didn't interfere with it."

Qing visualized the map. "Erguniang Peak? That's not too far from here. Which side of the wind array is it on?"

"Both." At Qing's raised brow, Li Tang added, "The sect itself is outside the array. But the array crosses about a third of the mountain on the far side from the sect."

"Would it be possible to dig a tunnel through to the other side?"

Scoffing, Hou San demanded, "Why would they do that?"

"To get through? What if they're Zhu Kan's allies...," A worse thought occurred to Qing. One he didn't like at all. "What if Zhu Kan killed them and replaced them with his puppets before you trapped him on that mountain? It was his stronghold, right?"

Both cultivators looked at each other. "Damn," Huo San muttered. "The boy makes too much sense. What are we going to do? Li Tang and I can't leave here. It'd weaken the array. We can send for help but we don't know how much time we have. We can't leave that nest of... whatever they are... to dig a way to free that bastard."

Really, there was only one thing they could do. "No one can tell what's inside these robes," Qing said calmly. "Or behind these masks. You send for help and the two of us go in to find out what's actually going on."

That and to find their masters, before Zhu Kan did something terrible to them.

修炼

Neither cultivationist liked Qing's suggestion. Neither had a better idea. As for Xinglu, he was perfectly fine with it, happily donning the biggest puppet's robes and putting on its mask. Of those remaining, only the robe that'd been halved was left for Qing, forcing a brief pause while Hou San sewed the thing back together.

"Try to keep to the shadows," she ordered once she'd put the finished product on Qing's shoulders. "The belt should hide the seam but I don't want you risking discovery."

Reflecting that he hadn't expected a woman of Huo San's personality to have the patience for sewing, all Qing said was, "I'll do my best, ma'am." He flattened the belt, tucking it in around his waist carefully.

Once they were properly garbed, Qing let Xinglu carry him on his sword, so he wouldn't have to turn fish and risk ruining his clothes' appearance. By this time it was quite dark, with only starlight to show the way to Erguniang. Fortunately, they both had excellent night vision, so the landscape was bright and clear, shining pale below them.

They arrived at their destination without incident, approaching a small plateau with a dozen or so buildings. They were small and neat, with well-tended courtyards, lit by a few small lanterns. No wall protected it, though, and there were no signs of guards or anyone else for that matter. Any intelligent bandit would look askance at such a lackadaisical approach to security. Perhaps the sisters were the innocent sort who didn't think they were in any danger, this far from the beaten path?

Landing out of sight of the buildings, Qing and Xinglu followed the trail to the gate and paused. Qing blinked at the symbol above the sect's name. A familiar symbol. The same symbol he'd seen back in Ziyou. But that was impossible, surely? How could Sanzan Sect's symbols be here? Of course, they'd never worked out how Ziyou City had gotten where it was, either.

A masked and robed figure stepped towards them, spreading their arms wide in welcome. A soft voice asked, "This one greets her sisters.

Was your mission a success?"

The voice was warm and gentle, exactly the sort of voice a kindly sister of a reclusive order should have. Qing hesitated. He was almost certain the person at the gate was another puppet. But she acted like a normal human, even if she neither smelled nor felt like one.

He inclined his head, whispering, "This one is not permitted to discuss."

"This one understands. Please pass." The gatekeeper stepped to the side.

Although it seemed too easy, Qing moved forward, Xinglu close behind. As they did so, Qing deliberately bumped into the gatekeeper, feeling the hard edges of a puppet body. He didn't say anything, however, to see what the other would do.

"This one asks excuse. Has been rude. Please continue." The apologetic tone startled Qing. Could a puppet really react in such a human fashion?

Once they were a decent distance away, Xinglu demanded, "What was that about?"

"It's definitely a puppet. Beyond that, I'm not sure." Qing had suspicions but until he'd a better idea of what was going on, he didn't want to jump to conclusions. "We'd best be more careful with those things controlling the puppets, though. There's something about them that worries me."

Xinglu thought about it. "You think Zhu Kan is using people to create them?"

That was exactly what Qing was afraid of. "If so, it'd explain why he's trying to capture me and Cui Wen. Why he'd take you and our masters, as well, if he realizes what they are." It was an ugly thought. One Qing desperately wanted to be wrong. "We haven't destroyed any of the orbs yet. Let's try to keep from doing so."

Because if they really did contain some essential part of a person's Self, he didn't want to be responsible for harming them.

修炼

The sect's halls were quiet, which was only to be expected. These puppets might or might not be what remained of Bingyuan's sisterhood but it was clear Zhu Kan needed them to create an image of normalcy. And normalcy demanded the sisters follow their routine of going to bed and getting up early. Likely there were all sorts of activities they followed by day, but at night the only ones awake should be whoever was in charge of securing the place and those who worked under her command.

Those particular puppets weren't easy to evade. They were, however, easily fooled. The masks and hooded robes Qing and Xinglu wore were sufficient disguise to get them past the guards for most of their exploration.

It was when they had to go down into the basement, following a faint odor of clay and stone that they ran into a more difficult guard. Taller than the others, more aware than the others, she, or it, stood in their way and refused to let them past.

"Go back to your rooms, sisters."

Xinglu set his hand to his sword, clearly ready to fight, but Qing stopped him. The guard at the gate had let them through because their answer had been what it'd expected. Would this one accept a facile answer the same way? He bowed, saying, "We have important information for the Sect Master. She is this way, is she not?"

The big guard paused. Tilted its head as it apparently tried to think. Then, finally, said, "Information of what sort?"

"Regarding the spirit beasts we were sent to capture. One carried a Book Hunter's tool." It was a calculated risk, letting them know what sect he belonged to, but given the symbol on the entranceway, he thought it a useful one.

Another moment of consideration. Then the guard stepped to the side. "Enter then. It's late. Do not disturb her longer than you have to."

Qing sighed with relief as he walked through the wooden door. His suspicion about this place was growing more certain, though he'd no idea how it'd come to be. As he entered the tunnel into the mountain, the guard whispered, "Good fortune, Sect Nephew. Free us."

Before he could speak, she closed the door between them.

修炼

"What was that about?"

Qing frowned as he paid close attention to the sounds around them. Nothing much yet, but he thought the floor and walls vibrated with a rhythmic thumping. "I'm not sure."

"You have an idea, though. I'd rather not be surprised by some strange revelation in the middle of all this."

Qing had to admit his friend was right. "I told you Zang Shanghu used to be part of a tri-part sect. One that broke up because one of our sibling sects, Zan Jing'ling, went rogue and started acting against Khaitan's government." At Xinglu's agreement, he continued, "Did you see the symbol right above the signboard for this place? That was our symbol when the three sects were still together."

"So you're saying these people are descended from one of your old sects? Except they aren't people. I haven't smelled a living creature since we came. Except us, obviously."

Xinglu being part spirit beast, and a fire hound at that, meant his sense of smell was a great deal better than Qing's. "More puppets, then." Qing wasn't surprised. He went on with the explanation. "That city I mentioned a while back? It used to be ruled by Zan Jing'ling's male side. And this one appears to be the female."

"You mentioned how they kept themselves separate. And, if I remember correctly, the male side collected spirit beasts while the female handled spiritual plants, like golden bamboo and silverleaf trees."

Agreeing, Qing continued, "Ziyou hid away inside that mustard seed space I mentioned. From the looks of things, the female side of Zan Jing'ling hid here. As harsh as things are, it'd be the last place in the world one would look for a collection of spiritual plants."

"I certainly wouldn't think to find them here," Xinglu admitted. "So you think that woman called you Sect Nephew because you're a member of a sibling sect? Or at least of a group that used to be the sibling sect?"

It seemed likely. "I'm not sure how she knew I wasn't one of them, but what I really don't understand is how a puppet could possibly be able to ask? More and more I'm afraid there's real people involved in those things."

Xinglu considered that. "I'm training in alchemy," he noted, "So I'm no expert in machinist skills. But do you remember what Zhu Kan did to the Song Clan? How he sucked out all their *qi*?"

That revelation had made Qing understand why Song You had been vengeful enough to wipe out Zhu Kan's descendants. The fact that Cui Wen's father and family hadn't had anything to do with Zhu Kan's crime apparently didn't matter to her. "I remember."

"What if those spheres we keep finding contain a bit of the soul of the life they came from? Maybe Zhu Kan found a way to dilute his victims' spirits so they're spread out among more than one puppet?"

That... that was the terrible thought Qing kept having. One he hoped was wrong but feared was right. "We should be careful. Don't destroy the spheres if we can help it."

As Xinglu agreed, they noted they were coming to the end of the tunnel, towards a brightly lit opening onto a familiar scene. "I was right about the city," Qing muttered, making sure not to speak around any of the other inhabitants of this place. There weren't many but they were all dressed alike and all moved in silent unison, going about their business like the puppets they probably were.

Xinglu glanced towards the pagoda at the center. "Then their collection of spirit plants would be there?"

"Likely yes."

"We should try freeing them later."

That'd have to be a great deal later after they'd figured out where their masters were. Not that Qing expected to find them here. Not with so much territory surrounding Yaomei Peak. His main hope was for a way past the wind array.

A moment later he blinked, reflecting that he really wasn't good at fortune telling. Just when he'd been sure they'd no expectation of finding their masters, there the pair were, peacefully wandering the city as if they were courting.

Which, knowing Master Zhi, was surely nonsense.

Chapter 7: Discovering Dangerous Truths

It was dark by the time the broken-off chamber landed, the howling wind outside chilling Zhi Wenku to the bone as she struggled to recover her equilibrium. Shen Wei joined her before she rose, checking her pulse. "Are you hurt?"

"Nothing permanent. My dignity is more battered than my body." Zhi Wenku had thrown up several times during their spinning trip and she was damned glad she'd gotten most of it out the window. "You?"

"I broke my second best fan and have entirely exhausted my patience with Zhu Kan." Shen Wei helped her up and offered her a drinking gourd full of something warm and nourishing. At her raised brow he noted, "I don't handle fasting well, so I always have food on hand. Xinglu won't let me keep the sweets with me, though. Claims I'd eat them all in one day. He isn't wrong."

She laughed, though it wasn't easy finding humor in their situation. "Where are we?"

Shen Wei examined the horizon. Frowned. "Somewhere on Erguniang Shan. And before you ask, this isn't the mountain Zhu Kan is imprisoned on. That's over there." Shen Wei pointed west at a dark silhouette against the evening sky. "Yaomei Peak, once his stronghold, now his prison."

A high wind blew from the base of Erguniang Peak, rising straight into the air in a way Zhi Wenku knew was impossible. "That's the prison barrier?"

Frowning, Shen Wei considered the wind thoughtfully. "Those involved in imprisoning Zhu Kan belong to a different branch of the Soul Protection Society. I don't know their methods, but I think this is just the first protection. I'm willing to bet there's another, primary array, surrounding his stronghold."

"How the hell did he drag us this far?"

"Might I remind you that I'm an alchemist, not a sorcerer?"

True. Zhi Wenku didn't deal with sorcerers often herself and couldn't pretend to understand half of what they did. She paused to check her Warehouse, making sure it'd taken no damage from the shaking they'd just gone through. Warehouses were tough, though, built to withstand a great deal. She smiled to see it was fine.

Tapping the communication tablet attached to her Warehouse's side, she asked, "Young Master Cui. Miss Shi. Are you two all right?"

"Everything's fine, yes. Ah, do you mind if we make some dinner? We're getting hungry and I notice there's a kitchen."

"That's what it's there for. Don't get into the blue-green box. That's for special occasions."

Once the boy had agreed, Zhi Wenku returned her attention to Shen Wei. "I'm sure Zhu Kan thinks we're trapped up here and I'm sure he thinks he has a plan for how to deal with us. I'd like to prove him wrong on every count, if you don't mind."

"My dear lady, I'd be charmed." Shen Wei led the way outside, adding, "I'm glad you sent Qing out, though I should mention that Xinglu is a great deal stronger than he appears."

That was good. "If we can't find an escape, we have backup."

They stepped out onto a snowy broad and flat surface. Too broad and too flat. Off to the side was a cliff covered in ice, the pale blue substance reflecting the light from Zhi Wenku's luminous night pearl and looking for all the world like the entrance to a temple.

It took Zhi Wenku a moment to realize there actually was a door. She eyed it distrustfully, then searched out the edge of their plateau. "Can we fly down from here?" she asked Shen Wei.

"Not so close to the sword-fall array." Shen Wei lifted a hand over the edge of the cliffside and showed how his sleeve fluttered, caught in a powerful gale that would have knocked him over if he hadn't been braced for it. "You wouldn't happen to have another way of getting down?"

Before Zhi Wenku could answer, something scraped behind them. When they turned, they saw a white-haired woman dressed in pale blue-white robes stepping thru the icy door into the cliff.

She was a strangely beautiful but unnerving sight. Her robes covered her entirely, so even her hands were hidden beneath the sleeves. As for her face, that was hidden by a porcelain mask. "This humble servant of Bingyuan Sect suggests the best way down is inside. Perhaps benefactors would be willing to consider it?"

If there'd been a simple way down from the mountain, Zhi Wenku and Shen Wei might have refused. There wasn't and the only ways either had were complicated by the fact that it was late and growing later. The night air was intensely cold. Even knowing they faced a trap they both chose to risk it.

They followed the woman through the doorway into a gleaming and intensely beautiful passageway. Zhi Wenku had once visited a glacial cave in the north and this had a similar remote and tranquil feel to it. There was an unexpected floral scent to the air, one that made Zhi Wenku want to breathe deep and take everything in.

She didn't. She'd been in enough situations like this to know how often it turned out to be fake. Drawing on her training, silently repeating the Book Hunter's Creed - 'Seek truth from facts' - she trailed behind the woman and hoped Shen Wei could protect himself from whatever was happening here.

"You don't seem surprised at guests," Shen Wei said, fanning himself with a new fan. This one had the same spell as the other, so words and images could appear at his command. To her relief, those words showed he understood their situation: 'Incense drugged. Induces cooperation. Take my pill.'

Zhi Wenku inclined her head. She'd thought as much. Tripping, she allowed Shen Wei to catch her and help her stand. "I'm sorry," she told the woman leading them, "The floor is a bit slippery." At the same time she accepted the pill Shen Wei slipped her.

"This humble one understands. It takes some that way." The woman continued on, though she somehow noticed when Zhi Wenku raised her hand to put the pill in her mouth. "You are unwell?"

"Our flight here was a bit rocky," Zhi Wenku explained, forcing a burp. "I'm rather afraid I was sick on the way." A complete truth and one confirmed by the stains on her robe.

The woman accepted the explanation, serenely leading them onward.

At the same time the elegant and austere passage they passed through faded as Shen Wei's pill took effect. Zhi Wenku's dizziness passed and her head cleared.

She focused on their surroundings, seeing how the ice covering the entranceway gave way to grey rock and bricks of dark brown clay. The lights changed too, going from the soft internal glow of the ice to flickering lanterns.

As they stepped out into a large chamber full of familiar looking buildings, Zhi Wenku raised her brows, recognizing the architecture and layout immediately. This was a perfect match to the mustard-seed city she and Qing had visited just a month back.

She corrected herself. Not a perfect match after all. Ziyou's citizens were a chaotic blend of human and spirit folk, all freed from the control of Zan Jing'ling sect by her fellow Book Hunters. This city was what Ziyou had been before that time, with only a few dozen sect disciples going about their business. The sound was different, too. Quieter, except for a faint rhythmic thumping in the distance.

Shen Wei's fan showed new words, 'You know this place?'

If Zhi Wenku had a fan like Shen Wei's she could have answered the question easily. Instead she spoke aloud, saying, "It's almost like being beneath a lake." She'd told Shen Wei the story of their adventure in Ziyou. It wasn't a secret and the sphere containing the place had long since been returned to Khaitan.

'So another hidden place?' At her silent agreement, he added, 'But under Zan Jing'ling control.'

The last wasn't a question but she confirmed it anyway. At the same time she slowed, pretending to gawk at all the fine buildings. The fine and nearly useless buildings, given how few people there were here. All female, unlike Ziyou City, which told her which group this had to be.

Their guide turned. Gazed at them with false patience. "Would you like a tour?"

The offer startled Zhi Wenku, then she realized the woman was waiting for that drug to take full effect. She inclined her head. "That'd be appreciated," she agreed. "If you don't mind."

The more time they had to escape, the better.

修炼

" SO ANOTHER HIDDEN PLACE ? "

They'd circled around the main street twice, their guide patiently waiting for the two of them to succumb to the drug's power. As they did, Zhi Wenku and Shen Wei watched for a chance to escape. Zhi Wenku was about to make her move when she noted they were being followed.

The pair behind them were dressed like everyone else but something about their build seemed wrong. Their movements weren't quite right, either; more like men disguised as women and unsure how to shift their hips. She realized why a moment later and glanced sharply at Shen Wei.

'Yes,' his fan told her. 'Our wayward boys.'

Well, that was good. She nudged the strap of her Warehouse, inclining her head towards the pair trailing behind them and received a sweet smile in response. Shen Wei turned his fan so their disciples could see the words. 'Are those children going to ramble behind us all night?'

Their disciples twitched. Shuffled embarrassedly in a way that was sure to get them noticed. Deciding it'd be best if the boys went elsewhere, preferably with the Warehouse, Zhi Wenku asked their guide, "I keep hearing a thumping in the distance. I hope nothing's wrong?"

"We are always working to improve our circumstances," the guide said quietly. "No need to be concerned."

"That sounds fascinating," Shen Wei offered. "I wouldn't mind taking a peek."

"It is not allowed."

"Ah. Ah, well. Our curiosity will have to be left unsatiated for the moment." Zhi Wenku sighed, deliberately looking drowsy. "I don't suppose my partner and I could be allowed to refresh ourselves before we meet your leader. It's not as if there's anywhere we could go unnoticed."

A moment's hesitation. Then, "That can be arranged. You did say you had a difficult trip." The guide led them through a doorway and Zhi Wenku paused to set her Warehouse down just outside the door.

She trusted the boys would know what to do.

修炼

Inside the building, Zhi Wenku gave her companion a sharp glance. Now she'd had a good look around she was certain these people had been the female led spirit plant collectors of the Zan Jing'ling. The question was, were they still?

It wasn't possible to tell anything about the people beneath the robes. They moved like humans, but they never did anything other than walk around aimlessly. Were they puppets, like the stone soldiers sent by Zhu Kan? And if so, what was their purpose here?

Stepping away from Shen Wei to draw their guide's attention, Zhi Wenku hoped her companion would understand her intentions. He quickly proved he did by striking the woman across the back of the neck in a way that ought to have knocked her unconscious.

It did not. Instead, their guide drew her sword, automatically coming to her own defense. She spun around, striking out in a sudden and oddly stiff move, paying no mind to Zhi Wenku.

That last was strange. Strange and familiar. Years ago, when she'd rescued Qing and his prince from those two puppets, the one had focused entirely on one target. A self-aware fighter would never turn their back on their enemy. They might as well be asking to have that back stabbed. Zhi Wenku swung her whisk, wrapping the hairs around their guide's body, holding her still.

They stepped back and forth, struggling to out-maneuver the other. At the same time Shen Wei watched for a chance and swung his fan, the edge cutting their guide's mask in half so it dropped to the floor. "I thought so," he said, as a wooden framework surrounding a sphere of bright gold was revealed. He tugged it free, and the puppet collapsed in a heap.

"Another of those blobs?" Zhi Wenku asked, removing her whisk from the silent puppet's body.

"En. I believe so." Shen Wei deposited the sphere in his sleeve, adding, "I don't know that I want to destroy these. Not without knowing what they are."

He was right. "I almost wish I hadn't destroyed the one in Zhu Kan's puppet. It's not like it saved us much trouble."

Shen Wei shrugged off the semi-apology. "We'll worry about that later. For now, am I right in thinking the women's branch of the Zan Jing'ling sect own this place?"

"I'm certain they used to. What the situation is now is harder to guess."

Shen Wei stepped to the doorway and looked out, checking for signs that someone might come to their guide's rescue. "I think it might be safe to explore. If memory serves, Ziyou City's pagoda was another Space containing their Spirit Beasts. Can we presume the pagoda here contains this place's spiritual plants?"

It made perfect sense to Zhi Wenku. "Paying it a visit might not solve our problem or give us much information, given it looks like the Zan Jing'ling are still in charge here. Sort of."

"It's a place to start, at least. We're singularly lacking in clues at the moment."

Since he was right, again, Zhi Wenku gestured with her whisk. "Then by all means, let us investigate."

修炼

There weren't any guards on the pagoda, a fact that puzzled Zhi Wenku entirely. It surely contained the sect's most important treasures. Why would they do nothing to protect them? Was there a trap? Or was something going on that Zhi Wenku just didn't understand?

Standing at one of the eight huge doors entering the pagoda, Shen Wei pushed briefly. No response. He tugged at it. Still no response. "Locked tight," he grumbled, then grinned in the mischievous way of a partially reformed street urchin. He pulled a set of picks from his sleeve, saying, "Keep watch."

Since Zhi Wenku had been about to ask him to do that very thing while she picked the lock with her whisk, she just grinned back and let him go to work.

He was fast with those picks. Fast and skilled. A twist here, a lift there, a tilt to finish the job. All done in mere seconds. Zhi Wenku whistled softly, admiringly. She could have done it herself, yes, but not as quickly, nor so elegantly.

Another bright grin crossed Shen Wei's face as he gently pressed the door open. "My masters would be appalled," he admitted. "But I don't see a reason to neglect a skill simply because it has a questionable origin. Or questionable uses, for that matter."

"I quite agree," Zhi Wenku murmured, eyes ahead as she examined the door sill. Yes. As before, this one had the same array on it. Look through the door without crossing the threshold and everything would appear a simple temple entrance. Once they stepped past, they'd be in the sub-dimension the Zan Jing'ling used to contain their prisoners.

And Zhi Wenku was under no misconception on that point. The spirit beings - plant and animal - the Zan Jing'ling had 'collected' had seldom been willing participants. The claim that they were being protected might be true, but it took away the rights of self-aware beings to choose their own dangers.

She stepped through the doorway, Shen Wei close beside her, fan readied for a fight. No surprise to find it was. Two robed figures waited just inside the entrance, ready to stop any unauthorized entrants such as themselves. The pair startled into motion immediately. A halberd struck at Zhi Wenku, while a saber tried to take Shen Wei's head from his shoulders. If they'd been foolish enough to just wander in they'd have been badly injured or dead in seconds.

Instead they dodged sideways, one left, one right. To Zhi Wenku's great approval, Shen Wei left her a clear line of attack. She'd had other fights where a would-be partner tried to protect her or at least get to the fight first, getting in her way in the process. She couldn't count how many times she'd had to yell at Qing for that mistake.

Catching the halberd with her whisk, the strands twisting tightly around the haft, she let herself be tugged forward, redirecting the weapon's movement so it missed striking her. Before they could react, she struck the robed figure's belly with a closed fist.

A sharp gasp and a cry of pain was her reward. One she hadn't expected at all. She'd been sure everyone here were puppets, but this guard was clearly flesh and blood and female. She twisted around, evading the guard's blow and caught at the mask. Hmm. Maybe not flesh and blood after all.

The woman who glared at her furiously had green tinted skin. Her eyes were wider than a human's and a color no human born had ever possessed. Pale lavender with pupils so red it almost hurt to look at. "YOU BITCH!" the plant spirit snarled. "I'll kill you!"

Zhi Wenku disentangled her weapon from the guard's. "Shen Wei. They're not what we think. Disengage." She shoved her opponent further back, giving herself space in case the woman attempted to attack again. "Easy."

"Don't you dare 'easy' me!" Before the guard could renew her attack her companion set a hand on her arm. "What?""

"They aren't with the enemy. They're flesh and blood, not puppets." The second guard removed their mask, revealing androgynous and elegant features. Was it Zhi Wenku's imagination, or did the pale gold skin seem to be covered in petals of some sort? "They wouldn't stop fighting if they worked for Zhu Kan. They may even be his enemies."

Zhu Kan again. Just as they'd feared. "We didn't come here to fight him," Zhi Wenku admitted, even as the first guard scoffed. "But it seems like we may have to, given he's a bit too interested in our business."

The second guard bowed. "This personage is Yin Shaoyao, a child of the Peony clan. The noisy girl is Hong Qi, of the Wolfberry."

Zhi Wenku bowed in turn. "Zhi Wenku, a humble collector of books."

"And this one is Shen Wei, of the Soul Protection Society." Shen Wei's bow was just as inappropriately deep as Yin Shaoyao's, much to the Peony guard's amusement. "Might we ask to speak to those in charge?"

Before Hong Qi could object, Yin Shaoyao inclined his? her? their? head. "I think that would be for the best. We get little word of what's happening outside our sanctuary. I'm sure our leaders would want to know first. Hong Qi, stay here and try not to cause trouble. Please."

As the Wolfberry guard grumbled, Yin Shaoyao led Zhi Wenku and Shen Wei off.

修炼

Like the pagoda sub-dimension in Ziyou City, this place consisted of a broad plain of rolling hills and small forests. Unlike the other sub-dimension, it had an artificial sun. Zhi Wenku was momentarily puzzled but realized the plant spirits who lived here would have needed something of the sort. Quite likely it rained here as well, though she saw no sign of clouds.

To Zhi Wenku's surprise there was a small group of huts built further inside the sub-dimension, right beneath the branches of a huge old tree. Nothing extensive and built from wood clearly borrowed from the buildings outside the pagoda. "I wouldn't have thought your peoples would need such things."

Yin Shaoyao smirked. "That's for the humans." At Zhi Wenku's raised brow, they added, "It's a long story, but suffice it to say Zhu Kan didn't capture all of the Zan Jing'ling followers when he sent his soldiers here."

"What surprises me is that you allowed them to stay."

"They owe us for the privilege. Once we rid ourselves of Zhu Kan, we will make sure they repay their debt."

Something told Zhi Wenku the plant spirits of this place would be quite put out if the Zan Jing'ling failed to deal with them fairly. That, however, wasn't her business. "Then I'll wait until we've met your leaders to learn what, exactly, is going on."

Shen Wei waved his fan lightly, the words changing to 'Given they're willing to tell us anything useful.'

That made Yin Shaoyao chuckle and both Zhi Wenku and Shen Wei blinked at them, surprised they'd noticed the comment. Smiling, the Peony guard said, "I have a particular sense for magic, Master Shen Wei. And a great fondness for words. It'd be a surprise if I didn't notice your amusing, and very useful, little spell."

"And I'd be a fool to use that spell for any important communication," Shen Wei answered, smiling in return.

Reflecting that Yin Shaoyao could have hidden their knowledge and spied their guests, Zhi Wenku quietly added the information in the Peony guard's favor. Then she focused her attention on the problem at hand. "I'll be interested in learning just how all of this came about."

Yin Shaoyao gestured towards a large tree standing over the village. "Let me introduce you to our leader and get permission to handle the matter first." At Zhi Wenku's raised brow, they added, "He's quite old and set in his ways, Master Zhi. If we had him take charge directly it'd be days, possibly weeks, before we'd get anywhere."

Ah, yes. Zhi Wenku had forgotten that tree spirits - and this one looked to be at least a thousand or so years old - tended to be deliberate and slow. They didn't have time for that.

Leading them past the village, ignoring the bewildered stares of the women tending their small gardens, Yin Shaoyao came to a stop at the foot of the old tree. "Elder," they said quietly. "Listen." They set their hand on the tree's trunk, closing their eyes as they focused their thoughts and slowed their breath.

It took an hour before the tree finally answered, dropping a large fruit into Yin Shaoyao's hands. "He thinks you might be hungry."

By this time they were, Zhi Wenku admitted. Except, "We have two apprentices wandering around outside. The sooner we learn what you know, the better."

Yin Shaoyao led them to a nearby wooden table, gesturing for Zhi Wenku and Shen Wei to sit. As they poured tea, they continued, "You wanted to know how this came about."

"We mostly want to know what Zhu Kan is up to, but I've a feeling that amounts to the same thing."

A smile. "Indeed. Likely it does, though I can't speak as to Zhu Kan's plans. Not all of them, at least." Yin Shaoyao beckoned one of the human sect members over. "I need paper and ink."

As the woman hurried to fetch what they asked for, Yin Shaoyao continued, "You know this so-called protected area was created by the Zan Jing'ling. From the fact that you're a member of their allied sect...."

"Former allied sect."

"...Former allied sect, I'm sure you know the Zan Jing'ling were forced to flee Khaitan three hundred years ago."

"Five-hundred."

"It's been that long? Never mind. Doesn't matter. The point is, the two halves of the Zan Jing'ling separated, each blaming the other half for their banishment. The female side came to these mountains and built an underground city, using a fake nunnery to explain their presence. And for much of the time that followed, they continued as they had before.... Protecting, or pretending to protect, the plant spirits they already possessed and trying to find a way to return to Khaitan."

No surprise they'd wanted to go back. *Qi* and magic in the outer lands was harder to access and harder to use. It took a great deal more strength and knowledge for an outlander cultivator or sorcerer to achieve their goals. "And Zhu Kan?"

"About twenty years ago a stranger came to the sect and persuaded their leader he could help them return to Khaitan. The fact that going back wasn't the only problem wasn't considered in their excitement. He tricked them into accepting his bargain, then took the sect's disciples to transform."

Transform. A sick feeling hit Zhi Wenku. "All those puppets. They have human souls?"

"I believe so, yes."

The single flat word made Zhi Wenku tighten her lips, staring at Shen Wei. "Those spheres." Thank the Gods he'd suggested they not destroy the things.

"Probably," he agreed, looking just as sick as Zhi Wenku felt.

Yin Shaoyao was clearly puzzled. "Spheres? Forgive this ignorant plant, but, what spheres?"

"Have you destroyed any of the puppets?"

The question only made the Peony guard more confused. "We've tried to avoid that. And again I ask, what spheres?"

Zhi Wenku pulled the one she'd kept from her pouch and set it between them. "This. I found it near the head of the stone turtle Zhu Kan used to attack my apprentice and his. There was another in a badly damaged puppet. I crushed that one."

Even as she spoke, she felt a sharp surge of self-anger. If those spheres truly contained some portion of Zhu Kan's victims' spirits, had she done irreparable damage to the life within? She'd thought it was just a power source at the time. Now all she could do was hope the spirit it'd belonged to hadn't been aware.

Yin Shaoyao frowned thoughtfully. "The only way to be sure would be to go to where he's building his puppets. We haven't tried so far, not wanting to risk retaliation. Perhaps it's time."

If it weren't for the fact that they were clearly and deeply involved now, Zhi Wenku might have been content to leave this problem to Shen Wei's Soul Protection Society. But Zhu Kan wanted Qing, and that made him very much her business.

"How much are you willing to do?" Shen Wei asked quietly. "You and yours are safe enough here. You don't owe humans or the human world your help."

The Peony guard waved at the landscape surrounding them. "This is a false paradise. We survive here, yes, but we do not flourish. Resources are limited and we must regulate ourselves strictly. Cultivated plant spirits are almost always wild plants; such restrictions don't sit well with us. We all want out. We all want free."

By which Zhi Wenku guessed they'd been looking for a way to escape long before Zhu Kan had tricked their captors into cooperating with him. "In which case," she said, "I can promise to request right of return for you back to Khaitan...."

"No."

At Zhi Wenku's puzzled glance, Yin Shaoyao pointed out, "As you said, it's been five hundred years. Other spiritual plants will have taken our places in Khaitan by now. We can spread out in these lands instead. Our cultivation might be slower, but we're mostly willing to try."

"I'll have to talk to my leaders on that point," Shen Wei said. "They'll want assurances. But if you help us stop Zhu Kan I can promise his mountain at the very least."

A bright smile. "A most generous offer indeed, Master Shen. Allow me a bit of time to confirm with our leader. Once he has, we will hopefully be allowed to assist you in taking down whatever it is Zhu Kan is doing in his factory."

修炼

Zhi Wenku used their wait to find out more about Zhu Kan. They'd been so busy, so constantly in a rush here and there that she hadn't had time. Nor the inclination, to be honest. Aside from the collection of weapons and machinist manuals they'd found in the stone turtle, Zhu Kan's doings shouldn't have been of interest to her.

"What, exactly, did he do to the Song clan?"

"That's an interesting question. We'd always assumed he'd used some demonic cultivation method to suck his victims' *qi* dry. The remains all looked like they'd aged a good century."

There were definitely demonic cultivation methods that worked that way. "So you thought they were used as cauldrons?"

"Living energy sources for *qi*? Yes. That's what it appeared." Shen Wei nibbled at the fruit the old tree had given them. "We did notice none of the Gold Core cultivators or above still had their Cores. But we didn't make much of that. Cores usually shatter when their owner dies."

Zhi Wenku examined the sphere they'd found near the turtle's skull. "What do you think would happen if I passed *qi* through this?"

Shen Wei gave her a sharp and worried look. "That seems like a dangerous experiment. I wouldn't attempt it without plenty of protections. And we don't have the luxury of time to play foolish games just because of curiosity."

He was likely right and Zhi Wenku knew it. Still, "I can't help wondering if there's some small part of the owner's spirit still inside."

A sigh. "Zhi Wenku, my dear woman, that thing may be created using stolen Golden Cores but it certainly isn't one. I've helped repair a cracked Golden Core once. They're a great deal harder and you couldn't hold it in your bare hand like that."

Bowing to the alchemist's greater experience, Zhi Wenku put the sphere away. "We'll consider it later, then. I do want to know if there's something aware inside." Seeing her companion's dour expression, she added, "It's a terrible thought, the idea of being trapped in such a state."

"I... can't argue with you on that point." Shen Wei poured her more tea. "In the meantime, we have more important problems. I see our host coming back and they look pleased. I think we have the help we wanted."

Yin Shaoyao did indeed look pleased, though when they joined them they said, "The leader would rather not send our people in to attack." At Zhi Wenku's raised brow, they added, "He did, however, give me permission to act as your guide and assist you if there's a fight."

By which Zhi Wenku guessed the leader didn't want to risk drawing Zhu Kan's attention on their sanctuary. One plant spirit joining his enemies could be an outlier. A whole group would be a clear and obvious declaration of war.

"All right," she agreed. "Then let's go as soon as possible. The sooner we've dealt with this problem, the sooner we can go back to what's important."

Which, in Zhi Wenku's case, was searching for lost and stolen books. Not chasing a mad cultivator halfway across the country.

修炼

They had to argue with Hong Qi on the way out of the sanctuary. Not because she wanted them to stay, but she wanted to join them. In the end, Yin Shaoyao had to put their foot down on the matter, wrapping Hong Qi in twisted peony branches to keep her from following.

"I'm sorry. She likes to fight," they said as the three of them returned to the streets, all garbed in the robes and masks that hid the true appearances of the sect members.

"I do believe I noticed," Shen Wei retorted. "But the fewer of us to draw attention, the better."

They headed through the streets again, ignored entirely by the passersby. When Zhi Wenku remarked on the apparent lack of security, Yin Shaoyao noted, "The sorcerer, the one you think is Zhu Kan, isn't strong enough to keep watch through all his puppets. So he leaves them a small amount of self-control and only takes over when he has to."

That fit with everything they'd seen so far. "Do they have any awareness of their own, then?'"

"Possibly? We try not to interact too much. Best to keep a low profile. They don't interfere with us as long as we don't interfere with them."

"Understandable." There were a great many of Zhu Kan's puppets out here. If he ever did focus his attention on the beings in the pagoda he might well find a way to harm them. She'd no doubt the Zan Jing'ling sect had had safeguards set on the place to keep its prisoners from retaliating against them.

When she said as much, Yin Shaoyao agreed. "We'd been slowly eroding those protections inside the pagoda when Zhu Kan came."

Eroding and no doubt taking advantage of the chance. "Justifiably so."

Yin Shaoyao led them to a large and new looking building carved into the cavern wall, stone soldiers guarding the doors. "This was built soon after Zhu Kan formed his alliance with the sect leader."

"Getting in may be difficult," Shen Wei murmured. He gestured at the guards protecting the entrance. "I doubt they're as lackadaisical about security as the others."

He was likely right. Zhu Kan surely kept a closer 'eye' on these than he did the other puppets. Whatever he was doing inside was likely more important to him than the rest of the city. Zhi Wenku pondered the building's entrance and the four grey figures waiting at the door. So far they hadn't been noticed, but they'd no way to approach. Not when their target was carved into solid stone.

Oh, but wait. "What's the probability that they're expecting the two of us?"

Shen Wei considered that. "I'm sure our guide earlier was leading us around the city to wait for the drug to take hold. No doubt she intended to bring us here afterwards. I can't see Zhu Kan turning down more puppets."

Zhi Wenku removed her borrowed robes. "In that case, since they're surely expecting us sooner or later, why not make it sooner."

It only took Shen Wei a moment to understand and he removed his robes as well. "If they ask when we enter, you know what to say?" he asked Yin Shaoyao.

A chuckle came from behind their mask. "Of course. We've watched this lot for a while now." Taking the lead, Yin Shaoyao walked towards the entrance. "No guarantees, of course. I'm not an actor."

Given they were all the three of them had, there didn't seem to be a choice.

修炼

They had no trouble getting in after all. Just as well, because Zhi Wenku didn't like the looks of Zhu Kan's workshop at all. The last thing she wanted was to be forced inside, unable to fight back.

Beyond the doors to the workshop lay a single large chamber with a jade table at the center and a construction area to one side. The table was empty, a glass half-globe mounted at one end, its surface covered in talismanic writing. There were shackles midway down and more at the other end. Worse, a glittering needle hung from a metallic cord, aimed right about where a cultivator's Golden Core would be.

The table was obviously where Zhu Kan stole his victims' *qi*, likely using that needle. A closer look showed the cord rising up and over to a vat of softly glowing gold liquid. No doubt that was where the spheres were created.

All around the room's edges stood other tables, all with the same half-globe at the top, each with a partially constructed puppet lying upon them, being worked on by a half-dozen stone statues. No restraints, but they weren't needed, not for mere puppets.

Those puppets were built of wood and cloth, their heads mere wooden frameworks. No need for real faces here. Why bother making the things look human when no one would see?

Or, no, there was one puppet with a face, and a familiar one at that. The same face as the puppet she'd broken back at the turtle. No doubt this one was under Zhu Kan's control. Possibly it always was. She didn't know or understand how he was doing what he was doing, after all.

Knowing better than to seem interested, Zhi Wenku stared blankly ahead, as did Shen Wei. Meanwhile, Zhu Kan's personal puppet stumped closer, choosing Zhi Wenku for the dubious honor of being his first victim. He didn't bother talking about it, for which she was grateful. She didn't need to listen to his excuses or explanations.

She let him lead her towards that table. Let him pick her up and set her down. Let him lock shackle after shackle onto her wrists and ankles. As he reached to drag the needle down towards her abdomen she pulled her whisk from its hiding place in her sleeve. A flick sent the *kirin* hairs twisting upwards to tangle around the needle. Yet another flick tore it free.

At the same time Shen Wei struck, flash-stepping forward, fan slicing across the puppet's neck, decapitating it. The stone statues, the ones building the puppets, spun round to fight, but Shen Wei dodged and danced out of their path. Yin Shaoyao struck as well, a sword of petals and wood forming in their hand, blocking the stone soldiers before they could reach them.

Meanwhile, Zhi Wenku used her whisk to pick the locks on her shackles. Then she examined the needle, spotting familiar but unreadable talismanic symbols engraved on its surface. She frowned, wondering exactly what the thing was and how it worked.

"We could do with a bit of help over here, my dear."

Realizing she'd been sitting and staring at the needle for longer than necessary, Zhi Wenku carefully put it away, pinning the thing into a piece of cloth so it wouldn't get lost. Then she leapt from the table and set to striking down stone soldiers.

It was not an elegant fight at all. The stone soldiers didn't have much in the way of battle skills but they couldn't feel pain and couldn't be knocked unconscious. All the three of them could do was break the things' skulls and take the soft sphere of energy that kept them moving.

Knowing what the spheres probably were made the fight harder for Zhi Wenku. She didn't like hurting people who were already hurt. Didn't like damaging slaves forced to fight by their master.

She was trapped between a choice of evils. Harm her attackers or become just as damaged as they were. She had to choose her own safety, especially if they were going to stop the monster behind this mess. That didn't mean she had to like it.

She struck and struck and struck, sending energy through her whisk and shattering as many of the stone soldiers' limbs as possible. They were less dangerous that way, giving Shen Wei and Yin Shaoyao a chance to end their fight by removing their heads for them.

At last the fight was over. They dragged their opponents together to the middle of the room, carefully examining the remains for those spheres and removing them from the stone skulls.

To be honest, Zhi Wenku wasn't sure they were doing the right thing. But as long as the spheres remained attached to Zhu Kan's puppets their true enemy could use them. Hopefully he couldn't hear or see anything now.

As for the puppets being built, none had any spheres as of yet. Likely that was the last step in the process. The question now was, just how were the things being created?

Zhi Wenku headed for the tank she'd noticed earlier. More talismanic script covered the surface, prompting her to bring out her translator. "This is language is from pre-Khaitan," she told Shen Wei when he joined her. "Almost no one but historians ever bother with it. There's dozens of better tools for arrays now."

"Was that when Khaitan was fully in the world?"

Yin Shaoyao corrected him. "Khaitan formed to block Chaos energies from escaping into the world. It's never truly been part of your reality."

"Really? Is that why Khaitan's magic and spiritual energy is so strong?"

Before the pair could get caught in a history lesson, Zhi Wenku interrupted. "We need to stay focused, please."

Two embarrassed faces glanced her way and Zhi Wenku continued, "I'm beginning to think Zhu Kan has been stealing magic and spiritual items from Khaitan as well as your people. If so, that makes what he's doing my business after all."

That made Shen Wei chuckle. "My dear lady, you weren't thinking of leaving this job half-done and you know it."

He was right, of course. Once she'd gotten dragged into this mess there'd been no way in the Eight Heavens or Five Hells that she'd walk away. Qing wasn't the only one for whom curiosity was a driving trait. "No," she agreed. "Yin Shaoyao, would you be willing to assist us further?

Because it's high time we found out what Zhu Kan is up to."

Not to mention find their apprentices and make sure they didn't fall into the sort of trouble they couldn't get themselves out of.

A gentle, slightly dimpled smile. "My dear Master Zhi. I couldn't be more pleased to help."

Chapter 8: Falling into Trouble

Once their masters were out of sight, Qing hurried forward and caught the Warehouse by its straps. It was obvious what his master intended for him. Keep the Warehouse safe. Investigate that noise. Stay out of trouble. Of the three, the last was the least likely.

No fool he, Xinglu led them back into the shadows of an alleyway. "We should check on Cui Wen and Shi Huan first."

They'd been so busy with all the various dangers that Qing hadn't even considered what'd happened to their other friends. He had Xinglu keep watch while he went inside.

"Took you long enough. What in the world is going on out there?" Shi Huan demanded. "We've been waiting forever!"

Now that wasn't true at all. "It's only been half a day." Seriously, were all born dragons this impatient? "Are you two all right?"

Cui Wen looked up from the impromptu work table he'd set up in the eating room. Bits and pieces of a machinist's art were scattered around him and he wore a pair of magnifying lenses that made his eyes seem horribly large. "I'm fine. Aside, of course, from having to listen to Miss Shi complain."

"I don't like waiting and worrying."

Qing had to admit he shared Shi Huan's feelings. "I don't either. But it's safer if you two stay here for a while longer."

"What's going on? Could you at least tell us that much?"

Cui Wen added, "I admit to some curiosity myself."

Quickly, Qing described the situation. "We think the puppets are digging an escape tunnel for Zhu Kan," he finished. "Xinglu and I are going to investigate."

"Let me come out. I'll help. Cui Wen can't, obviously, but I can hide in your robes," Shi Huan demanded.

"Not yet." Qing remembered her insistence on attacking the stone soldiers back aboard the turtle. The last thing they needed was for a repeat of that. "If you want to see what's going on outside the Warehouse, follow me." Qing led her and Cui Wen to the observation chamber, showing them how to use the controls. "This is how we make sure our surroundings are safe if we've been in here a while. You can't do anything but if you talk into this, I'll hear you through my earring." He gestured at a web-like object stretched inside a wooden frame.

They considered that and accepted the instruction. "You be careful, then," Shi Huan ordered. "And bring us out if there's trouble."

Now that was something Qing fully intended to do. He just hoped it wouldn't be necessary.

修炼

The thumping noise came from the far side of the city, precisely the direction it'd be if someone were building a tunnel towards Yaomei Peak. Qing's sense of direction, as perfect as any fish's would be, helped him here. "Except where's the noise coming from?" As far as he could tell this area was just the same as the rest of the city.

"Here. I smell clay and dirt this way." Xinglu sniffed the air. Tilted his head like the hound he was. Pointed towards one of the buildings, leading them forward without hesitation.

Thankfully, there were no guards, sign no one expected trouble from this direction. Qing and Xinglu entered unchallenged, passing two puppets carrying buckets of rock. Once the pair were gone, Xinglu said, "I think you're right. They're digging a tunnel. And if you're right about the direction, which I'm sure you are, it has to be so Zhu Kan can escape."

Qing wasn't sure he was pleased that he'd figured out what was going on or worried that Zhu Kan would succeed. A little of both, really. He followed Xinglu further into the building to the room where the puppets had exited.

There was a rough staircase leading further downwards, one so recently built that it showed little signs of wear. "He hasn't been at it long. But I wonder how he managed to start?"

"The stone turtle, perhaps?"

Ah, yes. That was right. As long as Zhu Kan had that thing he'd been able to send his stone soldiers out. But that meant he could turn people to puppets without ever getting his hands on them. Not a pleasant thought at all.

They reached the bottom of the staircase and a dimly lit chamber

"WHAT'S GOING ON OUTSIDE THE WAREHOUSE..."

where rock had been piled for removal. Now here was another interesting question. Given he had so many puppets under his control, why was Zhu Kan only using a few to do his work?

The question made Xinglu frown thoughtfully. "He can't be all powerful. His stone soldiers could only follow limited orders. Maybe he can only command so many?"

Qing wished they had some better idea of what they faced. Wished they had a better idea of Zhu Kan's powers, for that matter. All they could do was keep moving and hope they could work out the truth in time. The last thing they wanted was for Zhu Kan to escape.

When they entered the next chamber, he realized escape might not be their enemy's first purpose after all. The pounding they'd heard wasn't someone building a tunnel through to Yaomei Peak. Instead it came from a group of puppets diligently mining ore that glittered with faint silver sparks, all being carried down yet another tunnel. This wasn't an escape attempt. This was yet another grab at riches, just like the one in Lian Village.

And this time there was no pixiu to eat the treasure before it could be mined away.

修炼

If they did what Master Zhi and Master Shen expected of them, Qing and Xinglu would have turned around and gone back to report. They considered doing so, but not nearly as long as they ought. But they'd been tossed around, forced to hunt through mountains and fight their way to this place. They were both of them tired of being at the side and not getting to do something, anything, to help.

They did have the sense to find a quiet place so they could consult with Cui Wen and Shi Huan, who weren't in any mood to go looking for help either. Cui Wen, in particular, felt they should continue investigating. "Honestly, it sounds like those two have their hands full with whatever's going on inside that city. As long as we don't try to get to Zhu Kan himself, I don't know why we can't investigate this illegal mine."

That was right. Qing had mostly forgotten that silver mines were strictly government business. That'd been why the mine owner back in Lian Town had been panicking over the silver that pixiu had eaten. He frowned thoughtfully, remembering another detail. "Do you think your grandfather might be the one who sent that pixiu?"

Cui Wen considered the question with a puzzled air. "Why would he? Once a pixiu eats a treasure it only gives it to its master - given it has one. If grandfather sent it, why would they need to force matters?"

As Qing reconsidered, Xinglu offered, "The pixiu might have been an accident. We know the mine owner had a backer. What if that was Zhu Kan?"

With a snort, Shi Huan demanded, "Why would he need so much silver, anyway? He's a cultivator. Silver's useful, but I'd think he'd be more interested in the spiritual stones in these mountains."

Likely he was, but, "He's obviously got a use for it or he wouldn't have a mine here."

"Maybe we should follow that other tunnel, then. See what he's doing with the stuff."

Shi Huan agreed. "Let us come with you this time. Cui Wen and I can help."

The idea bothered Qing. Shi Huan was a strong enough fighter, but Cui Wen was in that chair. He was about to say as much when the young man snapped, "I have weapons and I can protect myself. Don't you dare pretend I'm helpless."

"I was just worrying about getting your chair through," Qing protested. "The mine shafts...."

"You saw what it can do earlier!"

A sigh from Xinglu. "We know your chair can walk, but the footing's worse here than it was back at the mountain."

"The ground's more stable here. I'll be fine."

Qing hesitated. He understood Cui Wen's feelings. If he were Cui Wen's master he'd refuse out of principle. But Cui Wen knew machines best and Qing was fairly sure there'd be more of the things waiting inside that mine. For that matter, Cui Wen might have an idea of what to do about all those puppets.

Agreeing despite himself, he said, "Don't overdo things. If you're overwhelmed and can't fight, hide."

"I will." From Cui Wen's tone, it didn't sound as if he believed either was possible. He and Shi Huan took deep breaths, clearly steeling themselves for whatever they faced. "Let's go."

修炼

There was no point waiting for the miners to rest or eat. Puppets needed neither, continuing their work with mindless patience and endurance. That mindlessness acted in Qing and his companions' favor, however. The puppets didn't notice their presence; or if they did, didn't stop them from entering.

"It feels too easy," Xinglu complained. "Master says if you can just walk into a place you won't walk out as easily."

Oddly enough, Master Zhi said much the same thing. "Do you have an alternative?"

"Well, Shi Huan is small and can walk on the ceiling. And you can be a really tiny dragon-carp if you need to be."

By which Qing presumed his friend thought he and Shi Huan should spy out the land ahead. Cui Wen might be able to traverse the tunnels with his chair in walking mode, but he couldn't help making noise. And Xinglu was big and bulky and all too noticeable. The puppets might not be paying attention but that didn't mean they never would.

"All right. Shi Huan?" At her agreement, Qing shape-shifted to his natural form and shrank down to the smallest he could possibly be. He swam up into the shadows above them, squeezing into a corner and waiting for Shi Huan to join him.

As they flew ahead of their companions, Qing paid attention to the sounds and smells of this place. The only living things around seemed to be themselves and the small animals who'd taken refuge down here. The latter weren't doing too well. There was little food to speak of aside from each other.

The other smells were similar to Cui Wen's workroom. The sting of lamp oil. The bitter tang of rust. Heated stone and metal. Was there a machinist working back here? It'd make sense.

Qing and Shi Huan stayed close together, working their way up and down the tunnels. Yet another reason why their scouting ahead made sense. Gods knew exactly where Zhu Kan kept his work room hidden away.

"Look out."

Shi Huan's warning came just in time. Qing nearly drifted down a bit too far, just when a robed figure similar to each and every one of the puppets they'd met so far, entered the passage. This one smelled alive, but moved as stiffly as the rest.

Another scent drifted upwards. Food? Actual food. This was first time since he'd entered the place that Qing had smelled anything remotely edible. All those puppets had no use for the stuff, after all. No use for tea, either.

"That has to be a human being. They wouldn't eat, otherwise." A tiny growl escaped Qing's belly, reminding him that it'd been hours since his last meal.

The noise made Shi Huan sniff a bit louder than Qing liked. "Don't get ideas, little carp. I know your kind will eat anything."

Qing ignored the admittedly true accusation. This wasn't the time. "Shh," he urged, as they trailed the stranger through the maze of shafts.

They reached a peculiar chamber, a carved out sphere with part of a building embedded inside. The walls surrounding the building were an odd mix of wood and plaster and grey and black stone. As for the building itself, it looked like the inner wall of a house, its plaster surface cracked to reveal the straw interior.

A door, as normal as normal could be, stood open at the middle of the wall, revealing a workroom so like Cui Wen's, up to and including the tracks on the ceiling that Qing thought for a moment they'd returned there. But, no. This one was bigger. More elaborate. And Cui Wen's workroom didn't have a pale sphere stuck on a stick at the very center, its surface glittering softly in the lamplight.

That sphere drew Shi Huan's attention and she clung to the shadows above it, as if she meant to drop on the thing and steal it away. Qing followed, unsure of what she was up to, hoping against hope the she wouldn't draw the stranger's attention.

Luckily, the stranger was more interested in the tea brewing in a machine exactly like Cui Wen's. They poured a cup, sipping at the stuff through a tube of some sort, so they didn't need to remove their mask.

As Qing and Shi Huan watched, the figure noticed a light flickering in a device off to the side. With a sigh they touched a lever beside that light, saying, "What?" Their tone made their disdain for whomever they were speaking to obvious.

A familiar voice spoke. Zhu Kan, sounding sharp with anger and accusation. "Haven't you found them yet?"

"The stone turtle was almost completely destroyed. Its contents were long since rifled through. Perhaps the ones you captured have them?"

"Damnit. That Book Hunter keeps getting in my way. Where are our captives?"

"Being processed by now. I'll check their belongings once that's done."

The so-called captives had to be Masters Zhi and Shen. Qing almost panicked before he remembered that the pair had been fine earlier. He didn't think they'd be as easy to 'process' as all that.

"See that you do. Don't think to play games. You know what's at stake."

"I know. You don't have to remind me every time."

A dour laugh sounded. "Oh, but I do. I know how you chafe at my commands. How carefully you walk the edge of obedience. You may deny all you wish, but I know it was no accident that a pixiu found its way into my mine just before the silver could be brought to me."

A sigh. "I told you, I had nothing to do with that. Or with what happened afterwards."

"Of course not." Disbelief soared in Zhu Kan's voice. Nor could Qing blame him. He'd have no reason to send that pixiu against himself. From the sound of it, this person might well have hidden purposes.

"What possible good would it do me?"

"Perhaps you hope for release? Dream all you wish, child. The armor I gave you protects you, but it's also your prison. Die and your spirit becomes mine."

"FUCK YOU!"

Zhu Kan continued, "Dying isn't in your best interests anyway. Not if you want your family back. What's left of them, that is."

The voice went silent then, not because Zhu Kan had stopped speaking but because the robed figure had struck that lever again, a great deal harder and angrier than the first time. Growling a curse, the figure pulled off their mask and hood, revealing greying black hair and badly scarred features.

Then, to Qing's shock and dismay, they turned and looked straight at him. "Didn't your master teach you better than to eavesdrop, little fish?"

Qing cursed, unsure how the stranger had realized he was there. Spotting Shi Huan about to dive, he acted first, snagging her by the tail before she could rush at the stranger. "Fly," he gasped through a mouthful of hair and scales. "Fast!"

As Qing dragged the dragon backwards, something hit the wall just inches away. A net, missing him so narrowly he felt the breeze of its passing. The stranger smiled, a horrifying sight in a face so mangled. "There's more where that came from, Apprentice Qing. You and that little dragon come here this minute."

Being in no mood to obey, Qing dodged downward, dragging an unwilling and struggling Shi Huan along with him, protesting loudly, "Why are we running? We can fight her. We can beat her."

Her? How could Shi Huan even tell, given the ruin of a person hid in those robes? Qing ignored the young dragon's shrieks, dodging darts and nets as he rushed back down the tunnel. Steps sounded: Measured. Loud. And somehow always just behind them.

Damnit. This was not how this was supposed to go. Qing had no idea how the stranger had known they were there and no idea what they... she... wanted. It was obvious she was an enemy, though. She wouldn't be working for Zhu Kan, otherwise.

"Let me fight!"

"No!" Dragging Shi Huan slowed him down but he didn't dare let her go back. Not without better reason than belligerence. "No need. ESCAPE!"

"SHE TURNED MY FATHER'S PEARL TO A LIGHT SOURCE!"

Wait. What? That sphere was actually a dragon's pearl? Gods. Gods gods gods gods gods gods gods! Qing almost let her go after all. A baby dragon could lose their pearl and survive. Shi Huan had, after all. But stealing an adult dragon's pearl meant digging it out of their foreheads. Not necessarily fatal, but painful and destructive, even so.

No wonder Shi Huan had been attracted. No wonder she was enraged enough to fight. No wonder she was enraged enough to kill.

Turning and fighting was very much desired, but very much the wrong thing to do. They needed to get away and get help. It wasn't clear if the stranger was the one who'd stolen those pearls, but they couldn't take the chance that she was capable of killing two adult dragons.

With a burst of speed and strength he didn't realize he had in him, Qing enlarged. Grabbed Shi Huan's tail. And dragged her, kicking and screaming, back towards their friends.

修炼

"What in the world?" Xinglu straightened as Qing returned, Shi Huan still struggling to break free, still screaming curses. They'd lost the stranger some distance back but Qing was sure she'd be catching up all too soon. He twisted, flinging Shi Huan at Xinglu. "Don't let her run off," he snarled.

"I WANT TO KILL HER!"

Xinglu caught the young dragon and held her tight. "I'm sure you do, Shi Huan," he assured her. "But not until we know what's going on. Qing?"

As quickly as possible, Qing described what they'd seen and heard. "Shi Huan thinks the sphere was made with her father's pearl."

"NOT THINK! I KNOW IT WAS!"

"AND YOU'RE NOT HELPING!" he shouted back. By now he was in human form again, turning to face the way they'd come. A bit more calmly, he added, "The woman's following us. She knows who we are and she might guess you're with me. I don't think we can escape, but I didn't want to fight her on our own."

"Good," Xinglu agreed. "No point in having allies if you don't use them." He tilted his head, listening. Nodded grimly. "I can hear her coming, despite Shi Huan's best efforts."

"You and Cui Wen hide. I'll wait here with Shi Huan. Make it look like I can't drag her any further." It'd be true, too. Qing was already out of breath from their escape.

Xinglu handed Shi Huan back to Qing and drew his sword before stepping off into one of the side passages, entirely ignored by the puppets carrying silver out of the mine. At the same time Cui Wen hid in another passage.

"LET ME GO!"

"STOP FIGHTING ME!"

The measured steps of their pursuit continued, until the stranger appeared at the far end of the passage, scarred features amused. "Did you think it'd be that easy to escape?" she asked.

"I hoped," Qing snarled back. "Shi Huan, you don't even know she did it...."

"I DON'T CARE! NO ONE USES MY PARENTS' PEARLS FOR A LIGHT SOURCE!"

"Light source? Is that all you think it is? Silly little dragon. As if anyone would be wasteful enough to use a dragon's pearl for a lantern." The stranger moved forward, one foot dragging slightly. By appearances she ought to be an easy fight. Qing knew from experience how deceiving appearances could be. Master Zhi could still beat him into the ground with a single strike. He dragged Shi Huan backwards a bit further as the woman continued, "You and your parents aren't using the things anymore. Why make such a fuss?"

Really, it was almost as if the stranger wanted Shi Huan to rip her throat out. To be honest, Qing was horribly tempted to let his companion try. But not yet. Not until the enemy was in reach.

To Qing's horror, the attack came too quickly and not from Shi Huan. Instead Cui Wen slammed out of his hiding place at high speed, screaming the name of his family's murderer as he rushed forward. "SONG YOU! YOU'LL PAY!"

"Damn," Xinglu muttered as Qing realized why Cui Wen was so furious. "Do we all have a reason to kill this woman then?"

"I don't. Did she kill your mother or imprison your father?" Qing asked, releasing Shi Huan so she could go to Cui Wen's aid.

"Ah, no. That was someone else entirely."

Qing hadn't known he'd hit on Xinglu's past quite so precisely. "Oh. I'm sorry."

"No. don't be. It's already dealt with." Xinglu watched the fight, clearly deciding whether or not he and Qing were needed. "She's good."

So were Cui Wen and Shi Huan. Once released, the pair worked together better than one would expect. Shi Huan didn't have much power yet, but she used what she had to spit globs of water that slammed into Song You's face and half-blinded her. At the same time Cui Wen used the bladed weapons attached to his chair to stab and slice at his enemy's chest.

Unfortunately, Song You might be crippled and damaged but she was a great deal stronger and faster than she appeared to be. She dodged Cui Wen's attacks, arm-blades blocking his weapons before he could strike. She didn't seem to be bothered by the water in her face, either, just spit and shook her head and moved on.

Tearing her robe free, Song You revealed she was wearing a suit of glittering black armor engraved with a gold array that seemed to shift and change with every movement. She drew a weapon, a bladed ball of the same material as her armor, gleaming black and gold. Qing caught a flicker of energy from it; the same sort of energy as in those spheres.

As the weapon rose in her hand, spinning wildly above her palm, Qing couldn't help groaning. "That thing's too powerful. They can't win on their own."

"Why not? They're doing pretty well," Xinglu offered, resettling his grip on his blade and preparing to join the fight.

"That array has too much energy for them to get past." Qing slid between Shi Huan and Cui Wen; striking at Song You's feet, twisting at the same time, tripping her. If she'd been pretending to be injured and limping earlier, the attack would have been pointless; she would have just stepped past.

Instead, unable to raise her leg high enough, the woman tripped over Qing, giving Cui Wen a chance to stab at her side through a chink in her armor. She hissed as the blade thrust in, then leapt back, shifting her focus to Qing. "Little carp," she hissed, flinging her weapon at him. "You're still a baby!"

Qing struck the thing back with a bolt of lightning, the attack passing on to its master and sending her reeling backwards. She fell but rolled to her feet, clutching her injured side.

With a shriek, Shi Huan flung herself forward. Blood spurted from her side as the bladed sphere struck her, but she ignored the pain to slam into Song You, knocking her straight backwards against the tunnel wall.

Song You tried to roll with the attack but it was too fast. She struck her head against a rock before she'd a chance to brace herself, the sound of the blow a wet squelch. A moment later she fell, struggling weakly against Shi Huan's grip. At last, fighting to the end, she went still.

修炼

Xinglu and Qing had to act fast to keep Shi Huan from ripping their enemy's throat out. "There's still questions to be asked," Qing told Shi Huan. "And she might have the answers."

"Besides, she doesn't smell healthy," Xinglu pointed out. "Never eat humans who smell like that. It'll make you sick."

They all looked at him and he spread his hands. "What?"

Deciding a half fire-dog spirit wouldn't understand the concept of not eating human beings, Qing checked Song You over. The blow to her head might not be fatal, though it hadn't sounded at all good. The deep stab to her side was a different story. She'd only remained standing through sheer cussed determination.

"Let's get her back to her workroom."

Cui Wen frowned. "Workroom? She has a workroom?"

"I'm assuming it's hers," Qing admitted. "It looks a lot like yours."

"But Song You isn't a machinist." At Qing's shrug, Cui Wen obviously decided to wait. "Right. Workroom. Let's go."

Qing and Xinglu carried the unconscious woman between them while Shi Huan - muttering under her breath at the idea of keeping Song You alive - led the way. All while puppets walked past them, going to and fro about their business.

"Am I the only one bothered by the way they ignore us?" Xinglu asked.

"No. But what are we supposed to do? Try and get their attention?" To Qing's mind it'd be stupid to set off a trap they could easily avoid.

Xinglu admitted he was right, "It still feels wrong."

By this time they'd reached Song You's workroom, only to have Cui Wen come to a complete halt, staring at the wall and flooring outside the room. "This can't be!" He pushed his chair forward rapidly, coming to a stop just barely inside, staring around in clear and unadulterated shock.

"This... this is my father's workshop!"

That made Shi Huan turn on him. "Why would your father have my father's pearl for a light source?"

"I... I don't know." He moved closer to the sphere, staring at it curiously. "I don't know what this is but it wasn't here before. I swear it."

Qing interrupted. "Shi Huan, we don't know exactly what happened to your father, but...."

"Aside from his being dead! Probably dead! And mother's probably gone too!"

"Yes. Aside from that. But we don't know for certain who killed them. We don't know how or why your father's pearl came to be here. But I'm sure Cui Wen had nothing to do with it."

"I swear I haven't, Miss Shi."

"Then give me the pearl!"

A pause. A worried look at the sphere. "I think that'd be dangerous. I don't know the half of what it's doing, but it isn't just a light source. As soon as I know how to get it free safely, I promise, absolutely promise, to give it to you."

Shi Huan hesitated. Sighed, curling around the staff holding the sphere in place. "All right," she agreed. "But you better keep your promise."

"I will."

Now they'd avoided another fight, Qing and Xinglu set Song You down on the floor. "Let's see if we can get her conscious." They needed answers and it seemed like Song You was the only one able to give them.

"I don't know if we can," Xinglu admitted. "Not without my master's help. I don't have the right sort of pill on me."

"Isn't she dead yet?" Cui Wen demanded.

"If she was, we wouldn't have bothered bringing her here," Xinglu pointed out. "Didn't we agree we wanted to at least question her?"

They settled Song You in a seat, binding her injury as best they could. It wasn't easy. That armor of hers seemed welded to her body. Certainly there were no visible fastenings. In the end they wrapped a cloth around her waist so she wouldn't bleed out.

Looking at the woman's horribly damaged face, Qing muttered, "She's been living a rough life."

"She's been on the run for what she did to my family," Cui Wen pointed out.

Fair enough. "Shouldn't she have been executed? What she did was murder, wasn't it?"

"I'm sure they would have. But someone gave her a chance to escape and she took it." Cui Wen eyed the woman's hands, adding, "From the looks of it, she's survived at least a dozen attacks since."

"A score," Song You muttered suddenly.

"Congratulations," Cui Wen growled. "Your run of luck is over."

The woman managed to look at him blearily. Frowned. "You are?"

Shifting his chair closer, moving so rapidly Qing feared he'd kill the woman out of hand, Cui Wen grasped her chin and made her look at him. "You shattered my meridians, ruined my cultivation. Or don't you remember?"

The woman's expression shifted. Almost seemed guilty. She still said, "The little crippled boy.... I could have killed you instead."

Before Cui Wen could react, Xinglu gently made him release their prisoner. "She's trying to make you kill her," he said. "Just like earlier, when she taunted Shi Huan."

It hadn't even occurred to Qing that that might be the case. He almost questioned his friend's belief, but Song You's lips tightened in a way that made it obvious Xinglu was right. "But why?"

"Look... at... me...," Song You growled. "At... what's... left of me...."

"Still doesn't make sense. We heard you earlier. You're working for Zhu Kan...."

"WHAT?"

Qing glared at Cui Wen, who quieted, a face full of grievance warning that it wouldn't be for long. Well enough. "You're working for Zhu Kan for your family's sake. If you die, won't that doom them?"

Now it was Song You whose expression held grievance and rage and frustration. "I've long since stopped believing he can do anything. It was a fool's hope, anyway, his pretending he still held their souls in his hands. His pretending he could return them to me."

A strange thought occurred to Qing. "Those spheres." He turned to Xinglu. "We were thinking those spheres were people once."

A weak incredulous croak. "Spheres?" Song You stared at the thing Xinglu took out of his bag. "That is?"

"We think it might be part of someone's core. Or made from their spirits. Or something. Bingyuan sect's disciples are all puppets; all controlled and powered by these things."

Coughing roughly, Song You managed to lean forward to spit blood on the floor. "Puppets? They're all puppets... that... explains... explains so much." More blood struck the stones, the woman's whole body shaking.

"Your father's work, boy. Now you see why... he... why all of you... had to die?"

Once again Cui Wen tried to reach out. Once again Xinglu stopped him. "My father never!"

"This... isn't his... work?" Song You reached into her belt pouch. Tossed a brass object to the floor. Pointed. "That's part of the machine Zhu Kan uses to steal his victims' spirits! Look at the mark and tell me it isn't your father's!"

Qing picked up the device, a hollow tube of heavy brass. The mark Cui Wen had identified as a fake version of his father's engraved on its side. He handed it to Cui Wen, who'd gone dead white at the accusation. "Is it?"

Breath held tight, teeth biting hard on his lip, Cui Wen used the magnifier on his glove to examine the mark more carefully. Then, with a sigh of desperate relief, he said, "No. This isn't his. It's like the one on the turtle."

"You... you're lying...."

"I know my father's mark as well as I know my own. This isn't it. It looks the same, but it isn't engraved right."

"He's writing it wrong on purpose then!" The woman's rage made her spit more blood and she fell back in her seat weakly. "He has to be the one..."

Was she fighting the truth out of stubbornness? Or was accepting it too much, given what she'd done to Cui Wen and his family because she'd mistakenly believed Zhu Jianhong was behind her family's death? Quietly, Qing asked, "If he is alive. If he is writing it wrong deliberately; doesn't that mean he isn't willingly involved? I mean, a maker's mark is an act of pride. Of ownership."

A groan escaped the woman's throat. A faint whisper of words impossible to hear. Qing started forward. Stopped himself. Master Zhi was always saying how impetuous he was. Song You might be trying to trick someone to get close enough to harm. He opened his mouth, intending to warn the others, but Shi Huan slithered up the woman's arm and put her head close enough to hear.

Only a few more words passed Song You's lips. A few words and several more mouthfuls of blood. Then nothing more, as the woman slumped in her chair. Shi Huan looked up, "She's unconscious. We're not getting anything more out of her."

Cui Wen gnawed at his lip. "What was she saying?" he asked Shi Huan abruptly.

"She said, 'Wrong. Everything wrong. My sins come back.'" Shi Huan turned a confused look on Song You. "She also said 'Wasted'. I don't understand what she meant."

Neither did Qing. He was about to say so when he felt the air shift in the room. He looked towards the door where they'd entered and was startled to see only a blank wall. "What?"

They all followed his gaze. Stared. "Where's the exit?" Shi Huan demanded. "What happened? Cui Wen, what is this?"

The boy shook his head. "I don't know."

"This is your father's workroom."

"It was," Cui Wen agreed. "But my father's workroom was in Yunnan. I don't know how it even got here."

Qing turned around and spotted another passageway through the opening on the eastern wall. "Look."

Again they followed his gaze. Again they gaped. The opening beyond revealed an old hallway, half-broken apart and clearly disused for years. Cui Wen whispered, "That's home." He was about to hurry towards the opening, but Xinglu stopped him. "It's just home!"

"You don't know that. And even if it is, it's been abandoned since Song You murdered your family. Do you really want to go back to that?"

Cui Wen sagged. "But how did we get here?"

"I don't know," Xinglu grumbled. "But I don't want to risk getting lost. Did one of you touch anything?"

They all denied it. "We've all been focused on...." Another shift of air and the hall into Cui Wen's old home was hidden by a wall. At the same time another opening appeared off to the side, this time leading into a passage more like the one they'd entered by. Except it wasn't the same opening. Worse, there were stone soldiers standing guard here.

"Take them out quickly!" Qing shouted, but he was too late. One guard struck a lever on the wall beside him, flooding the workroom with a swirling pale gas.

Qing held his breath, hoping against hope to outlast the drug. As his sight faded and his knees gave way, he knew he'd failed.

Chapter 9: A Storm of One's Own Choosing

What part of 'those children are always in trouble' did Zhi Wenku not understand?

In truth, she should have sent them back out of this place. Should have taken Qing and Xinglu's ability to fall straight into the hottest pot of water into account. Worse, she feared Shi Huan and Cui Wen shared that unfortunate talent. How else to explain the four of them finding their way into an illegal silver mine and straight into a battalion of stone soldiers?

Dodging below a stone sword, muttering curses, she was mildly amused by the words on Shen Wei's fan. 'Like masters, like apprentices?'

"Doesn't explain the baby dragon or machinist," she pointed out.

"Well, no." Shen Wei smashed his attacker into the ground, attacking with his sword for the first time since they'd met. "But those two likely have other excuses."

True. Zhi Wenku wrapped her whisk's strands around her attacker's neck and sent it flying into the wall, shattering it. This was the tenth she'd destroyed, with another ten falling to Shen Wei and a dozen or so to Yin Shaoyao. There were only a few more ahead, but the question remained; how had their apprentices gotten past this lot?

At last they reached the end of the passage, a hollowed out and mostly empty room that didn't seem big enough to contain so many stone soldiers. At her complaint, however, Yin Shaoyao pointed out, "They don't breathe. They'd fit if they were packed in."

"Hmm. Yes, I suppose so." Zhi Wenku scanned the room while Shen Wei examined the only thing in it; a staff with a pearlescent sphere glowing atop it. "Do you know what this is?"

"Unfortunately not." Shen Wei continued his examination, carefully avoiding touching the thing. "Do either of you two see where our young fools have gone?"

"Not yet." The room was a near perfect hollowed out sphere. Only the paving stones beneath their feet were flat. "I think these were added later," she muttered. "But why?"

"There's dirt beneath," Yin Shaoyao noted, fingers reshaped to roots, exploring the cracks between the stones. "Perhaps this room was carved into a perfect sphere?"

That made sense but begged the question why? Surely whomever carved this room could have left a proper floor when they'd done so? Zhi Wenku continued her exploration. "The stone's different from the passageway. And there's an opening covered by more stone."

Shen Wei straightened from his examination of the staff. "Are we sure the children came this way?"

The first thing Zhi Wenku had done when she'd taken Qing as an apprentice had been to set up two tracking arrays. One to point out his direction, the other to follow his path. Given his talent for getting himself entangled in peculiar messes, one couldn't depend on a direct route being possible.

She held up her compass. Frowned. "It's behaving oddly." The needle pointed back the way she'd come, as if somehow she'd missed the change in direction. Perhaps she had?

"But there's nowhere else to go," Yin Shaoyao protested as Zhi Wenku followed the needle to the entrance. When it swung back the way she'd come, the Peony spirit added, "What's happening?"

Passing the compass back and forth between the passage and the chamber, Zhi Wenku's frown deepened. "I don't understand myself. It's as if the path ends here." A cold chill washed over her. Were the children dead? To reassure herself, she shifted the compass spell to point in Qing's direction.

"Thank the Gods," she gasped. The needle aimed east, the dim light at its tip telling her just how distant her foolish little dragon-carp was from her. "But how?"

"A transportation spell?" Shen Wei's uncertainty didn't help. "Something to do with this sphere?"

"Have you figured it out yet?"

"I'm an alchemist, not a jeweler," Shen Wei sighed. "There's something inside this globe. Familiar, but I'm not placing it."

Zhi Wenku and Yin Shaoyao joined him. "It's a dragon pearl," the Peony spirit said suddenly. "I remember the master of the beast spirit collectors had one."

A dragon pearl? "Shi Huan's?"

"You said she's a youngster, right? This one's far too strong for that. Bigger, too. And filled with *yang* energy, so likely a male dragon's."

Lips tight around her emotions, Zhi Wenku finally said, "I think we need to activate this thing. Find out what it does. It wouldn't surprise me at all if that silly carp of mine touched something he shouldn't have and got himself transported."

A faint dour smile flickered. "If not your carp, my wolf." Shen Wei set a hand on the globe and turned it, setting the thing glowing a brilliant opaline shade. The glow spread, filling the chamber, setting it vibrating.

Without warning, Yin Shaoyao collapsed.

修炼

Qing wriggled. Twisted. Forced himself to full consciousness.

Not that it helped much. He lay curled in a glass jar, his side aching where something - a stone foot? - had kicked him. He'd changed to his smallest form but failed to escape his captor's notice. For the second time in as many days he was trapped.

This time he could see what was going on outside his prison. Stone soldiers and puppets passed by; some carrying crates of silver; some carrying crates of gold glowing spheres; some watching over crucibles filled with molten metal. Those last were familiar, puppets wearing the same face as the one in the stone turtle. Zhu Kan?

Scanning the room, Qing spotted a black dog chained up against one wall and another jar containing Shi Huan. Both were deeply unconscious; or seemed to be. He couldn't depend on them for help, not given their condition. Worse, there was no sign of Cui Wen, which worried Qing badly. "No time to waste," he muttered to himself, examining his prison.

It was worse than that gourd. Glass, which meant his lightning wouldn't damage it. Covered in protective arrays, which meant he couldn't break it by enlarging. Heavy, which meant he couldn't roll it off the edge of the table.

Qing's movements drew one of the puppets' attention. "Little carp's woken up first. Good. Good." The puppet drew close to Qing's prison, leaning down to look at him. "Such a brave, bold, little monster. You've put so much effort into cultivating. Have you enjoyed stealing my power from me?"

Stealing? Zhu Kan's power? Or... wait. "Those puppets back then, when I'd just cultivated. The ones who tried to catch me. They were yours?" How could he not have realized the connection until now? He should have known whomever was behind those two wasn't going to give up. It'd been years though.

"Clever little monster." The old man's face came closer to the jar, peering at him with satisfaction. "You used up a whole spirit stone on yourself. Too bad you'll never have a chance to grow further."

Used up? This man, puppet, whatever, thought Qing had used up that spirit stone? He'd be dead if he had. It'd taken Master Zhi's seal to slow his absorption rate. It'd taken months of training afterwards to transform the *qi* he'd already absorbed to a proper beast core. And it'd taken months of struggle to avoid cultivating all the way to dragonhood before he was prepared for the tribulation it required. Surviving the energies of the transformation would take everything he had.

He didn't bother telling the old man any of this. Just glared at him grimly. He was helpless, but he yearned to do something, anything, to strike back at his captor. Angry, frightened, desperate; he automatically loosed his lightning, letting it crackle through his prison in a brilliant display.

" FOR THE SECOND TIME, IN AS MANY DAYS,
HE WAS TRAPPED. "

The old man flinched back. So, Qing noticed, did the other puppets bearing his face. That was... interesting. Possibly useful. But not useful yet. He had to break free of this jar somehow.

The old man checked the cork. Chuckled. "Little monster, you've no hope of escape. No hope of rescue. The path here is secured. Even if your so-called masters find their way here, they'll have to fight through all my soldiers to reach you. By which time, I promise, you and your friends will all be absorbed into my plan."

Absorbed? Qing was certain the man meant that literally. He was certain those spheres were what they'd feared. Not golden cores; they were too weak for that. But related, though he couldn't guess how. Not yet.

Rather than give Zhu Kan an audience, Qing curled up into a ball, hiding his face from his captor. Amused, the man patted Qing's prison. "Don't worry, little monster. I'll be making use of you soon enough."

The old man turned away, leaving Qing to contemplate his escape. He had to and he had to do it before the old man could make good on his promise. Qing had no doubt his master was coming after him. No doubt she'd find him sooner or later.

The trouble was, he didn't think he had time to wait.

修炼

They knelt beside Yin Shaoyao, checking the Peony spirit's pulse. Checking their meridians. "What is it?" Zhi Wenku asked.

A whisper; weak. Breathy. "My... roots.... Can't feel my... roots."

"We've been transported too far from their plant," Shen Wei murmured. He pointed out the southern opening, adding, "Look."

Turning. Looking. Zhi Wenku saw half ruined rooms through the opening. A glance east showed her another room, this one in no better state than the first. "What is going on here?" she asked, holding Yin Shaoyao's hand, offering support.

"I'm not entirely sure," Shen Wei muttered. "I've heard that Song You had been working on an array that could switch two sections of the world with each other. But she'd never willingly work with Zhu Kan."

Song You. The name was familiar. "That's the one who killed Cui Wen's family, avenging her own?"

"That's right."

"The key word is willingly. Master Zhu has shown a talent for forcing people to help him who wouldn't otherwise." Zhi Wenku slid Yin Shaoyao's hand into Shen Wei's and went to the eastern opening, then the south. "I'm checking to see if our young fools have been wandering in this mess. But, no. The dust's too thick. They'd leave prints."

"We really should switch this thing back where it was, then," Shen Wei suggested. "I don't know how long Yin Shaoyao can handle being separated."

True. A glance at Zhi Wenku's compass confirmed the choice. "That foolish child is nowhere near us, anyway."

Shen Wei handed Yin Shaoyao back to Zhi Wenku and set off the staff again, transferring the chamber back to its previous position, or so Zhi Wenku expected. To her surprise, "The southern passage is closed."

"And the eastern open," Shen Wei agreed, as Yin Shaoyao managed to sit up, hunched forward in a slightly less wretched state. "You're better now?"

"Still too far from my plant to do much," Yin Shaoyao told him. "I... can stand. But I don't think I can fight. How useless."

Zhi Wenku squeezed the Peony spirit's hand. "We never asked you to fight our battles. That you've done as much as you have is appreciated." She looked at the compass, then pointed at the eastern opening, where a new passage had opened up. "We're a great deal closer now. Are we inside or outside of the prison array, do you think?"

Shen Wei waved the question off. "I don't think that matters. We need to go after those children and now we can."

They could, but they'd have to leave Yin Shaoyao behind. The Peony spirit could barely walk, much less follow along. As for fighting? Not a hope. "Will you be all right here?"

"I'm weak. Tired. But I can still protect myself. You go. I won't say I'll be all right, but your children need you. That's a thing I understand."

Having no choice, knowing the sort of things Zhu Kan was capable of, Zhi Wenku joined Shen Wei, walking into the eastern passage, every sense sharpened as they entered their enemy's lair.

They'd barely gotten a few feet away when the chamber behind them suddenly flared with light and disappeared. Or, rather changed from the room they'd been in before. Instead, a wall appeared, a few feet in from the opening, a mechanist's workroom just visible past a makeshift doorway.

A woman in a suit of armor, black leather and steel, stood in the center of the room, gauntleted hand set on a device just like the one in the other chamber. She stepped towards them. Stumbled, blood pooling at her feet.

"Song You?" Shen Wei said quietly. "It's you?"

The woman—Song You—spoke; straining, gasping, desperate. "Help..

help...stop...me. Don't... let... armor... take me. Please. Please. Begging you... please."

Zhi Wenku faced the armored figure, lips tight, eyes grim. The plea was heartrending but how could she trust when a bladed sphere rotated above an armored hand, clearly prepared to fight? Was Song You lying, or was the real enemy the armor she wore?

And, in truth, would it ultimately matter?

修炼

With Zhu Kan's attention elsewhere, Qing slumped in the bottom of his prison, trying to think of an escape. He'd just proved how useless his lightning was against the glass walls. If he were stronger, closer to his next stage of cultivation, he'd have a chance. Right now he was still too weak.

Or, wait. There was a way. A risky one. Master Zhi would be quite annoyed with him, but if he undid the seal that slowed his absorption of *qi* from his spirit stone, he could access the energy he needed. The trouble was, could he handle it?

He'd almost exploded himself when he'd first eaten that spirit stone and become a dragon-carp. Was he strong enough now to control the flow until his seal could be restored? Or would he blow himself up trying?

If he thought Zhu Kan would give his master time to come to the rescue he'd have waited. He was supposed to wait, not impetuously use his powers without using his common sense. Waiting wouldn't work now. Not when Zhu Kan meant to turn him and his companions into power sources for whatever cruel, mad, scheme he was up to.

Making up his mind, Qing settled into place, curling up in the bottom of the jar, focusing his attention on the seal. The pattern of thought needed to undo the thing was complicated, deliberately so, giving him plenty of time to change his mind. He did not.

An image formed around Qing, a rotating sphere of words in a language not spoken anywhere anymore. The script was even older, coming from another culture entirely. All written in Master Zhi's own *qi*, almost too painful to touch and almost impossible to erase.

He did it anyway, ignoring the dull ache that became burning soreness that became sharp pain growing sharper. Master Zhi had told him, 'I won't make it impossible to undo. But it'll be difficult. The most difficult thing you've ever done. So make it worth the pain.'

It was worth the pain, he reassured himself and her. More than worth it, because his life wasn't the only one at stake. Word after word faded and the pain grew worse and worse, until he was struggling desperately to breathe. If he lost hold he'd have to start all over again. He wasn't sure he could.

Then the pain ended and a new trouble began. Breaking the seal released the spirit stone's remaining energy all at once. Not as much energy as before, quite a bit less than he'd realized, but still more than he'd had to deal with since the day he'd cultivated into a dragon-carp.

Now he struggled to keep control of the flow, letting the energy increase inside him, letting it transform him, pushing him further and further towards the next stage. Lose control here and he'd be destroyed, not just sent to the beginning to try again. Lose control here and he'd be fish paste spread all over the inside of the jar.

He held on somehow. Held on and absorbed and grew. And grew. And grew. Not physically, that would injure him. But his cultivation increased, pulsing through his meridians and flowing through his *dantian* in a rush. When he'd first become a dragon-carp, the flow would have been impossible to manage. Impossible to bear.

Qing's years of cultivating under Master Zhi's tutelage gave him the strength to hold on and the strength to control all that energy. It wasn't easy and it'd only take one mistake to end his attempt, but his confidence grew each moment.

The flow slowed to a trickle and faded. Yet he could feel the change in strength, could feel his *qi* pressing against the bottleneck. It wasn't strong enough to break through, but he was so close, so very close, that it would only take a bit more *qi* to get him there. He'd used up his spiritual stone in the process but that didn't matter.

What did matter was the fact that he was strong enough, just barely strong enough, to do what he couldn't before. Drawing his lightning together, he focused it towards the weakest part of his prison, the glass stopper at the top.

Then he let it rage.

修炼

Song You stumbled closer, reaching out for Shen Wei. Only a quick-step to the side and a sweep of his fan saved him from being caught. Distracted by the man's sudden motion and defense, their attacker turned just enough to give Zhi Wenku a chance to snag her whisk around the woman's neck. When Song You jerked sideways, attempting to break free, Zhi Wenku went with the motion, sending *qi* through the strands of her whisk to bolster her attack.

The woman crashed to the ground, flailing around weakly in an attempt to rise. Zhi Wenku didn't give her a chance, catching hold of her wrist, spinning her around onto her belly, arm twisted behind her back in a position that would have held a normal human in place.

This wasn't a normal human. Or, rather, the normal human wasn't in charge. Her wail of pain as her arm twisted made that clear. Something inside the armor snapped; bone or cartilage, Zhi Wenku couldn't tell. She leapt backwards, giving Shen Wei room to dodge inside Song You's reach, searching for the armor's straps. Nothing.

"How do we get this off her?" Zhi Wenku demanded. "Before it kills her and us?"

Shen Wei kept the woman's attention on him. "If it's what I think, the straps are hidden underneath. Use your flail."

Understanding immediately, Zhi Wenku flicked the strands of her flail's whisk, snaking them between Song You's arm and her bracer. Using her *qi* to feel what she was doing, she found the bands holding the thing onto the woman's arm and cut. The black metal clattered to the floor.

"Keep the armor occupied," she ordered tersely.

"Of course."

By now Song You had fallen silent, eyes rolled back in her head, lips gnawed bloody. Had she fainted? Died? It didn't matter and wouldn't until they'd removed the rest of that damned armor and gotten to the heart of the matter.

Piece by piece, Zhi Wenku divested their attacker of their armor, kicking the pieces away as they fell to the floor. Bit by bit, Shen Wei forced their attacker to her knees. And, at last, the armor no longer in control, he lowered Song You to the floor.

They knelt beside her, wiping blood from the woman's mouth and trying to rouse her. At the same time Zhi Wenku asked, "This is the woman who killed Cui Wen's family?"

"It looks like her. I met her once, when she was brought in for trial. She escaped, but at a cost." He indicated her face and the lacerations crossing her cheeks and down her throat. "The binding net won't damage what doesn't struggle."

The implication was clear. Song You had broken free, paying for her freedom with damage that must cover her whole body. Zhi Wenku didn't bother asking more, examining the woman. Not that she had much hope. Song You was in horrifying shape. Thin as a wraith, dry skin like something long dead, the only sign of life was a slow and thready pulse. And, to make things worse, a stab to the gut that still leaked blood.

Sitting back on her heels, Zhi Wenku sighed. "I don't think I can save you, Shen You."

"Already... already did... as much as possible.... Broke that bastard's armor."

"Was that what I think it was?" Shen Wei asked. "Binding armor?"

"Yes. Forced... me... to obey.... Carried me wherever *he* wanted... Used... pain... *qi*...."

Zhi Wenku had never heard of such a thing. But based on their fight, she had to believe it. She also couldn't be distracted. "Who's the master? Zhu Kan?"

"Yes."

"Did he have you do something with some children? Three boys and a young, very young, dragon?"

A sigh. "Saw them... The dragon... blamed me for her parents being lost... the one boy... for what I did to him and his family. Can't... blame him... even if... he killed me."

By which Zhi Wenku guessed the stab wound had been Cui Wen's work. "Do you know where they are?"

"By now? Could be imprisoned... could be... being added to... master's power source."

Added to Zhu Kan's power source? Oh, that was not good at all. Zhi Wenku tightened her lips. "How do we get to them?"

"Can't... fight him...."

"Cultivator Song, we have no choice. Two of those boys are our apprentices," Shen Wei noted. "You don't have much time. Please don't waste it on warnings. How can we find them?"

"We're... in the bastard's fortress. The part... outside the shield. Head... for the lowest level... closest to his power source...." Another sigh, this one followed by a series of bloody coughs. "Good luck to you.... You'll need it."

Then silence, as the woman finally died.

修炼

The glass cork shattered into dozens of pieces, cracking the glass jar in the process. Qing startled, curling up on himself, half expecting the shards to pierce his soft hide. Except the few that struck him bounced off painlessly. He glanced at himself, seeing how thick and strong his scales had become.

Oh, he was close, so very close, to breaking through. His enlarged core was almost full; just a bit more spiritual energy would send him past the edge. This wasn't the time, though. He couldn't risk increasing his cultivation here and now. Not when doing so would draw down his first tribulation.

Noting that the shards had stopped falling, Qing slithered up and out of the jar, hoping against hope no one noticed his escape. It was a vain hope. There were still several of Zhu Kan's puppets here and whatever they saw, he saw.

"Just where do you think you're going?"

Evading Zhu Kan's puppets, Qing sped towards Xinglu. Broke his chain. Poked him. Nudged him. Loosed a small thread of lightning that startled his friend into confused awareness. "Wha?"

"Get Shi Huan out of here," Qing ordered. "I'll keep Zhu Kan distracted." He twisted in the air, spinning around to dodge between the puppets towards the only doorway. They followed him, or most did, and he rushed through, only to find himself hovering over thin air.

The hell was this? Qing scanned his surroundings; a deep hole, surging with *qi* energy, surrounded by a stone walkway. A faint glow above drew his attention and he flew closer to examine it. A curved wall of blue and gold light, marked with symbols Qing didn't recognize.

"You can't cross that, fool carp!" the puppets all yelled at once. "You'll die if you try."

That had to be the prison array keeping Zhu Kan from leaving his mountain stronghold. Qing wasn't sure why the sorcerer didn't want him dying but suspected it'd make him useless as a tool.

He turned his attention back downwards, spotting a long curved ramp working its way down the hole. Faceless puppets carried boxes of those golden spheres down towards a faint light at the bottom. Something told Qing that was where Cui Wen had been taken.

Master Zhi would have wanted Qing to escape. Would have wanted him to wait for help. But he'd no idea where she was nor how long it'd take her to find him. Cui Wen might be in danger or might be forced to work for his grandfather. Whichever it was, Qing needed to know where he was and how to save him.

He dove down, ignoring Zhu Kan's puppets' shouting, ignoring their effort to chase him. They couldn't keep up and they couldn't stop him. Not when he could fly. Not when he could draw on the *qi* in this mountain fastness and push himself to his limit.

Within moments he'd dropped down into a large chamber, scanning it quickly. On one side lay a melon sized blue stone embedded in the floor. Two adult dragons - shrunk small, their pearls pried from their foreheads - dug at its base. Across from the pair, a half-dozen puppets poured those gold spheres into something resembling a furnace. Towards the center was a mechanist's worktable where Cui Wen crouched over a metallic object resembling a hand. And in the center, lying still and silent on a huge table, was a giant puppet wearing Zhu Kan's face, one arm incomplete, its chest wide open and empty.

As Qing landed, he shifted back to his human form. "Cui Wen," he called. "What's going on here?"

Startled, the boy looked up, then glanced past Qing with an expression of horror. "Get lost!" he shouted. "It's not safe!"

The warning came a moment too late. Qing had landed between Cui Wen and the giant, thinking the latter unable to move. He was wrong. The thing stretched out its one arm, grabbing Qing by the waist and sending him flying across the room, smashing him into the wall.

Qing coughed up blood. Struggled to his feet. Glared at the giant as it stood. It lowered its head to look at him, a dry laugh echoing. "Fool carp. You can't escape me. I am everywhere."

"You might be everywhere, but you can only focus properly through one." The claim made the sorcerer snarl, confirming Qing's suspicions. Zhu Kan had spread his consciousness between all the puppets, but he couldn't fight with them all at once.

The puppet stalked closer, jeweled eyes glittering as he worked his completed hand. "I don't need more than this one, little fish."

The sorcerer was likely right. Qing's human form was soft and vulnerable. His dragon-carp form was too small. And though he had the Warehouse hidden in his sleeve, he'd no time to access it and pull out any sort of weapon. Not that there were any strong enough to deal with a puppet twice his human body's size. He and his master were Book Hunters, not warriors.

He glanced past the puppet at Cui Wen. No help from there. Zhu Kan had sensibly confiscated the boy's wheelchair and all his weaponry. Qing was sure Cui Wen was trying to work up some clever device to help, but he hadn't time.

The dragons - and they had to be Shi Huan's parents - had bands wrapped tight around their throats. Control devices, Qing was sure. Without their pearls they didn't have the strength to free themselves. Without their pearls, they were forced to obey Zhu Kan's will.

Shi Huan's mother glanced Qing's way. Flicked her tail. Flicked it again, drawing Qing's attention to the stone between her and her husband. Did she want him to do something? If so, what? Qing evaded Zhu Kan's puppet and examined the stone.

A spirit stone. Not nearly as powerful as the one Qing had swallowed, which puzzled him momentarily. But then, that was right, spirit stones outside of Khaitan were weaker than those formed inside his homeland's borders. This one was at least eight times as big as Qing's had been and contained only half the power.

Half the power was still a great deal of *qi*. More than enough *qi* to push Qing into breakthrough. The risk of doing so, without anyone around to help him if he lost control, was incredible. The risk of letting Zhu Kan get hold of him and finding some way to bind him or steal his power was far worse.

He reached out mentally, drawing on the stone's energies, sending them flowing through his meridians. As Zhu Kan's puppet caught hold of his throat, unaware of what he was doing, he forced the *qi* into his core, absorbing it and letting it carry him that last dangerous step.

An image of a river formed in his thoughts. A river and a huge set of rapids. The Dragon Gate, waiting for the next fool carp yearning for ascension. He'd been preparing for this moment for most of his life now. It was time to test his will and face his tribulation.

As lightning coruscated around him and into his attacker, all he could do was hope the bastard shared the risk.

修炼

A roll of thunder echoed through the halls of Zhu Kan's lower fortress. Echoed and rumbled through Zhi Wenku's bones. "Oh no."

"Qing? Ascending? I thought he still had a year or so?"

"He had a year or so if he didn't absorb all his spirit stone's energy at once." Even then the boy shouldn't have been breaking through. There was just enough energy left in the stone to get him close. Not enough to let him cross over. She would have made sure he couldn't break the seal on his own, otherwise.

When she told Shen Wei as much, he frowned. "This was Zhu Kan's fortress before it became his prison. I can't be sure, but perhaps he had a reason to build it so far from civilization?"

Not good. There weren't many large sources of *qi* outside of Khaitan but sorcerers and cultivationists did like to build near them. It hadn't occurred to Zhi Wenku that that might be the case here. "We have to find Qing. Stop him."

Stopping mid-step, Shen Wei set his hands on Zhi Wenku's shoulders. "My dear lady," he murmured. "You know as well as I do that that's not possible."

He was right. She didn't want him to be right but he was right. "Then let's at least find him and keep Zhu Kan from interfering."

They hurried on, following a well-worn path through a stone passage, one that opened out to a walkway surrounding a deep hole. The thunderous sound came from that way. Starting for it, Zhi Wenku was startled when a huge black dog and a familiar dragon burst through a doorway and nearly went over the railings guarding the walkway.

"Apprentice, what have I said about leaping before you look?" Shen Wei asked, tapping the dog on the head as the animal shook himself.

The dog whimpered, tail between his legs. Xinglu's beast form would have been impressive if he didn't look quite so much like a scolded puppy. "Sorry, Master Shen."

"The two of you are all right? Where's Cui Wen?"

"We don't know," Shi Huan gasped. "But I smell my parents somewhere near. And Qing ran off to distract that old bastard and there's a dozen puppets that look just like Zhu Kan and...."

"And stop." Zhi Wenku patted the dragon to calm her down. "I know where Qing is. Let's get to him and see if we can help."

They headed down the ramp, Shi Huan sitting on Zhi Wenku's shoulder, shivering a little with trepidation. No surprise. She had to be terrified for her parents, given what powered that transportation device of Zhu Kan's.

It took almost a minute to make it down the ramp, in part because the faceless puppets kept blocking their path. Not, Zhi Wenku noted, to defend it, but because they had a place to go and nothing would stop them.

At last they spotted the cause of the trouble and, as Zhi Wenku feared, it was Qing. He shifted between forms rapidly, bolts of lightning surging around him as he twisted and struggled in the hand of a giant puppet wearing a familiar face. Other puppets with that face tried to break the two apart, only to be shattered by the force of the energies surrounding the pair.

Shi Huan screeched wildly, spotting two exhausted dragons digging around a blackened and empty orb. "MAMA PAPA!" She flew at them, crying, trying to get their attention, before Zhi Wenku could hold her back. Ah well, hopefully she'd be safe enough, that far from Qing and his tribulation.

Cui Wen was there too, hiding behind a fallen table, peeking out once in a while then dodging back as a bolt of lightning crackled too close. Xinglu, nudged by his master, leapt off the walkway and curled around the boy, protecting him with his spiritual energy.

Zhi Wenku and Shen Wei had already set their defenses flowing around them. There wasn't much they could do but wait and hope.

It didn't take long, either. Whether by luck or training, Qing made it past his breakthrough with a final thunderous blast. Zhu Kan's puppet flew backwards, slamming into a furnace glowing gold with those spheres, shattering the thing as it landed. Sparks flew around the twisted frame, and Zhi Wenku would swear she heard a thousand voices screaming, the noise matched by Zhu Kan's shriek of pain and fury.

Then silence.

修炼

Qing roused slowly. Raised his head. Gazed around to find his master standing over him, her expression mixing annoyance, fear and pride. "On one hand, I distinctly remember telling you not to try breaking through until you were stronger and better able to handle your tribulation."

"Yes, Ma'am. Sorry Ma'am."

"On the other," A gentle hand skritched behind a newly grown horn. "On the other, I am impressed. Not many would think to use their tribulation as an offensive weapon."

"I wasn't sure it would work," he admitted. "But I thought it might slow him down."

Master Shen looked up from his examination of the furnace. "I think it helped. Though breaking this thing likely finished him." He stood, using his fan to point out the shattered pipe rising from the furnace. "I wager he was using this device to maintain himself inside his prison."

Did that mean Zhu Kan was dead? Qing hadn't seen what'd happened to the giant puppet, being too busy dealing with an entirely new and very different body from a fish's. He'd become accustomed to four legs at least, but he wasn't used to being so long, or seeing energy in quite this way.

"Mama! Papa!"

Attention drawn to where Shi Huan was trying and failing to get her parents' attention, Qing forced himself onto his feet. He knew what was wrong. Those binding collars were too much for the pair to fight. The mother had just barely been able to point out the spirit stone. Slithering closer, trying not to tangle himself up in his new tail and mane, Qing hooked a claw and sliced it across one band, then the other.

"A-Huan!" That was Shi Huan's mother, wrapping herself around her daughter and holding her close. The father was next, ignoring everything in favor of making sure his family was safe.

Seeing the three were curled up into a scaled ball of emotion, Qing returned his attention to the others. Xinglu, human once more, had picked Cui Wen up, much to the boy's annoyance.

"Don't grumble," Xinglu told their friend. "We need to find your chair first."

"We have quite a bit of clean-up to do," Master Zhi told them. "Give Shi Huan and her parents time to recover. We'll check the rest of this place out and make sure there's nothing else needs our attention. Qing, can you be human again, please? And I trust our Warehouse is safely put away?"

Changing to human took no time at all. Finding the Warehouse, fallen to the far back of Qing's *qiankun* sleeve, took a bit longer. By the time he had and handed it over, Zhi Wenku was tapping her foot and muttering about children who refused to clean their rooms.

"It's my sleeve. Not my room."

"It's still a mess and you need to organize."

Master Shen chuckled and whistled to himself as Xinglu flushed. No doubt this was a conversation they'd had with each other as well. Only Cui Wen, whose machinist training required organization, looked on in a puzzled way.

At last, Warehouse found and *qiankun* sleeve repacked, they climbed back out of the hole and set to exploring what they could of Zhu Kan's fortress. There wasn't much. Most of the place was hidden behind the prison array that kept Zhu Kan's living self contained.

There also wasn't anything left to fight. All the puppets had stopped moving. Some - the ones with Zhu Kan's face - had fallen over, their bodies charred as if whatever had powered them had burned away. The boxes of gold spheres lay tumbled on the ground, most of their contents dissipated.

"What happened to the silver?"

"Quite possibly moved past the barrier," Master Shen suggested. "I've a feeling we'll find a counterfeiting operation inside, once someone goes in to check."

"I see no reason for that someone to be us," Master Zhi noted, much to Qing's disappointment. At Master Shen's raised brow, she added, lips curving in the smuggest smile Qing had ever seen her wear, "Although, I suppose, as a Book Hunter, I should make myself available to examine any scrolls or books Zhu Kan might have in his library."

Master Shen's smile matched Master Zhi's. "Indeed," he agreed. "I'm sure the Soul Protection Society would welcome your expert advice and assistance. There's going to be quite a bit of work to do, after all."

Qing grinned to himself. He usually didn't enjoy sorting through messes and dealing with politics. But this time he had friends to help and mysteries to resolve.

And, now he'd finally become a true dragon, new powers to explore.

Epilogue

It took several months for Shen Wei to persuade his elders to allow the prison-array around Zhu Kan's fortress to be opened. It took several more months for the task to be completed. Ample time for Zhi Wenku to take her apprentice back to Khaitan to settle into his new status as a terribly young and terribly inexperienced dragon.

She took Shi Huan and her parents as well. They'd been badly injured by Zhu Kan's treatment and no one outside Khaitan's borders knew how to restore their pearls to their proper places. Even in Khaitan it took a dozen or so healers some time to help them.

This gave Qing a chance to learn from Shi Huan's parents. He'd been taught Khaitanese dragon culture, but if he was to travel outside with Zhi Wenku he now had to understand what his kind were allowed and prohibited there as well. Fortunately, he was a well-mannered youngster and eager to learn.

At last they returned to Zhu Kan's fortress; Zhi Wenku riding her crane, escorted by two adult dragons and two children, the latter squabbling genially all the way. Not that this was anything new. Qing and Shi Huan had long since formed that sort of friendship. Whether it would lead to anything in the future was something Zhi Wenku refused to speculate on.

Shen Wei waited for them in the courtyard outside Zhu Kan's fortress, his apprentice and Cui Wen waiting behind him. His fan flickered with images this time. Fireworks and blossoming flowers, an excellent match to his mood and Zhi Wenku's. "I've missed our talks," he told her.

"As have I. Elders Shi Feng and Shi Ming are good company but their daughter and my apprentice have kept them quite busy." Zhi Wenku folded her crane back into storage and cupped her hands to her fellow Master. "Have you entered the fortress yet?"

"I haven't, but the battle and sorcery arms of our sect went in already. They've cleared the building of traps." Shen Wei eyed the entrance, iron gates wide open to reveal a wall and a surrounding walkway. "A great many traps, it seems, though poorly maintained."

"And Zhu Kan?"

"His remains were at the center of the array he used to control those puppets of his. They look like they'd been struck by lightning." Shen Wei glanced at Qing, who was too busy gossiping with his friends to notice. "I believe your apprentice's tribulation found its way through the connection."

Just as well not to mention that to Qing. The boy only knew that his rise to dragonhood had stopped their enemy. Qing didn't like the idea of killing and would be bothered if he knew Zhu Kan was dead. Besides, Zhi Wenku didn't want him thinking of tribulations as a weapon. Someday he'd have to face another. Best not be tempted to force it.

"And the... ah... Bingyuan sect? And the spirit plants?"

"Yin Shaoyao has been examining the mountain to see if it'd do for a new home for their people. The Bingyuan... well, the ones turned to puppets are fading, now Zhu Kan's no longer maintaining the array. The others are assisting Yin Shaoyao in preparing a place for their former wards."

That was good. Zhi Wenku had expected the puppets to fade but she'd been concerned for the few survivors of Zhu Kan's attack. She'd no fondness for what Bingyuan sect, or rather Zan Jing'ling sect, had been, but she wanted them to change, not be destroyed. From the sounds of it, they were headed towards that end. A better fate than had met the beast spirit collectors of Ziyou City.

"Well then, since you've already been in and have surely mapped out Zhu Kan's library, perhaps you and your apprentice would escort us inside to do our part?"

A grin, quickly hidden behind Shen Wei's fan. "Of course. But first, a welcoming present." He held out a silk wrapped object.

Zhi Wenku couldn't help smiling, taking a package from her sleeve. "I have a gift for you as well," she murmured, to his obvious pleasure. "Hope you accept. Please, open it now?"

He did so with a gleam of anticipation that quickly turned to delight. "Is this?" The small box seemed plain and non-descript but at her guidance he set his finger on the seal, claiming it. Then he opened the box and entered it with a laugh of pure pleasure. "It is!"

"It's not much," Zhi Wenku admitted, joining him in the plain and mostly empty room. There were shelves because even the smallest Warehouse had to have shelves, but nothing else. "A Warehouse grows through its owner's cultivation. I'm sure it won't take you long to enlarge upon it."

Shen Wei's smile broadened. "This is already more than I ever expected." He glanced at the package in Zhi Wenku's hand, reminding her of his gift. "I hope it suits."

She opened it. Smiled as broadly as he. She'd never mentioned her admiration for Shen Wei's fan and the spell that let him project words or images on its surface. That he'd noticed anyway said much for his observation. She shook it out. Bowed. Projected the words, 'A pleasure to receive' and was answered with, 'A pleasure to give'.

"Master Shen!" "Master Zhi!" Two voices called them back to their duties, making them leave Shen Wei's Warehouse to lead the way into the fortress. As they did so, Zhi Wenku reflected that while she'd enjoyed being a solitary Book Hunter for years, having an apprentice, and now an excellent friend, was nice.

And, she hoped, a sign of a profitable and informative time to come.

THE END

ABOUT OUR CREATORS

WRITER -

BARBARA DORAN - has been making up stories for as long as she can remember. From playing Ms. Marvel to her best friend's Captain Marvel to writing new stories for old characters (Hannibal King, X-Men, Green Hornet, The Saint, The Shadow and many others), to writing gaming and anime fanfiction online.

After ten years behind the keyboard as a software engineer, Barbara realized that her true love wasn't coding but making stuff up. So when she left that career in favor of dealing with two frequent interruptions of her life (namely her own personal Tiger and Dragon), she decided to use what little time they allowed her to work on writing. Her Long Suffering Husband, without whom she could never have managed such a goal, has been nothing if not supportive.

Along with reading every mystery, SF and fantasy book she could get her hands on, Barbara grew up watching Star Trek, Batman, Green Hornet, along with the usual Saturday morning cartoons. She became addicted to shows like Battle of the Planets and Doctor Who in her teens and discovered Run Run Shaw's martial arts flicks some years later. Those influences, along with a love of folklore and mythology, have become part of the world some small portion of her mind lives in. When, of course, she isn't chasing Tiger and Dragon from one school event to another.

Barbara can be contacted at <BarbaraDoran@sumergoscriptum.com>. Her website is <http://www.sumergoscriptum.com/barbaradoran/>.

INTERIOR ILLUSTRATIONS -

GARY KATO – was born in Honolulu, in 1949. He graduated from the University of Hawaii with a Bachelor in Fine Arts degree. His comic book work has appeared in such varied titles as Destroyer Duck, Thunderbunny, Ms. Tree and Mr. Jigsaw. He's also illustrated children's books such as The Menehune of Naupaka Village and the currently available Barry Baskerville Returns and Jamie and the Fish-Eyed Goggles. He's also been a contributor to the Children's Television Workshop magazines, 3-2-1 Contact and Kid City.

COVER ART –

G.S.Davis - is an artist hailing from the wilds of Arvada. At the tender age of 15, he discovered that his calling was storytelling. Naturally he discovered this talent while trying to get out of trouble with his mother. As time went on, he evolved his talent and soon began writing comics. Now, many years later, he's still trying to avoid getting in trouble, though he believes that his wife is probably on to him at this point. So he tends to hide in his office, writing comics and putting them out into the world. He draws in two different styles: A cartoon style distantly reminiscent of the newspaper strips of yore, and a more serious Manga style, distantly reminiscent of Japanese comic books from that far away land.

Also from Barbara Doran:

www.ingramcontent.com/pod-product-compliance
Lightning Source LLC
Chambersburg PA
CBHW051134260626
47170CB00005B/1808